D1561371

BETTER BE TRUE

ANDY GALLO

ANYTA SUNDAY

Better Be True

Copyright © 2020 by Andy Gallo and Anyta Sunday

P.O. Box 1654 College Park, MD 20741, USA

This is a work of fiction. Names, characters, places, and incidents either are the product of author imagination or are used fictitiously, and any resemblance to actual persons, living or dead, business establishments, events, or locales is entirely coincidental.

Cover Art

© 2020 Cate Ashwood

www.cateashwooddesigns.com

Cover content is for illustrative purposes only and any person depicted on the cover is a model.

All rights reserved. This book is licensed to the original purchaser only. Duplication or distribution via any means is illegal and a violation of international copyright law, subject to criminal prosecution and upon conviction, fines, and/or imprisonment. Any eBook format cannot be legally loaned or given to others. No part of this book may be reproduced or transmitted in any for or by any means, electronic or mechanical, including photocopying, recording, or by any information storage and retrieval system, without the written permission of the Publisher, except where permitted by law. To request permission and all other inquiries, contact Andy Gallo, P.O. Box 1654, College Park, MD 20741, USA; visit www.andygallo.com; or send an email to andy@andygallo.com.

From Andy

For my husband Michael, for encouraging me to write and for allowing me to chase my dreams. And to 'lil q, my daughter, for keeping my life in balance. You both teach me the meaning of love.

CHAPTER ONE

Nico

Elisa: Need to speak to you ASAP. Emergency!!!!

Nico: Way too many exclamations. Give me a few I'm about to meet Tomas.

Elisa: Serious! Call Me! Huge Prob!!

Nico Amato shook his head. What was it about getting married that turned his normally rock-solid sister into a bundle of jittery nerves?

Would he be like that when he got married? One day. Maybe. Hopefully?

He palmed his phone into his pocket and thanked the guy who let him into the Pi Zeta Eta house.

A string of hollers met Nico's ears when he rounded into the lounge. He was immediately hit with the scent of Doritos, sweaty feet, and toxic masculinity. On the TV, some uniformed Hercules chased a ball.

Nico didn't recognize the team; didn't much care, either. He wasn't here for sport. He was here for Tomas.

His boyfriend.

His boyfriend of three months.

A record for Nico.

His lips curved at the sight of him, sprawled like a hot Italian god over an armchair. Nico had lucked out. Not only was Tomas hot, he was Italian-American and from New York. His nonna had approved when he'd told her he'd met someone.

She'd tried so hard to get a name out of him, but they were still so fresh, and he couldn't have Nonna noseying her way into Tomas's family when Nico hadn't even met them yet.

Maybe that was what Tomas wanted to chat about?

Summer break was practically upon them; maybe he wanted to know if Nico was up for meeting the 'rents.

His stomach hopped with nerves and hope.

Before Nico could speak up, Tomas's buddy nudged him and pointed toward Nico.

Tomas sprang to his feet so fast, Nico hid a grin.

"My God, Tomasso Merighi, you make my heart flutter just walking." He put his right hand on his chest.

When their eyes met, Tomas's body sagged.

So did Nico's good mood.

Tomas cuffed his elbow and curtly steered him out of the lounge. "I thought I said to text when you got here?"

"Your brother recognized me and let me in." Nico frowned. What the actual fuck was this about? "What's wrong?"

Fresh air hit them, and Tomas started pacing the porch before him.

Nico's stomach ached as he waited. He knew this awkward silence. He'd experienced it, oh, a hundred times before.

"We're . . . this isn't working." Tomas rubbed his nape, never meeting Nico's gaze. "I'm sorry. I think we should . . . you know. See other people."

"What happened?" Nico said, throat pinched. "I mean, we were good Thursday night."

"No, we weren't."

"So that was someone else I fucked after your frat party?" Tomas had been a bit drunk and insisted they leave early. The sex had been totally hot.

"That's not what I mean."

Nico's hands flew to his hips, and he cocked his head. "What *do* you mean?"

Tomas glanced up, brows furrowing. "*That* is what I mean." He gestured toward Nico's stance. "Everything is so dramatic with you."

"Dramatic?" Nico raised his hands and pointed toward his hips. "You think this is *dramatic*? You're breaking up with me. What do you expect? Roses and a sonnet about how wonderful you are?"

"No. It's just . . . You wore a shiny purple coat, eyeliner, and tight leather pants to a *fraternity* party. It was a kegger."

The picture came into focus, and its reality stung. "I embarrassed you in front of your bigoted frat brothers."

"They're not bigots, Nico." Anger flashed in Tomas's eyes. "They never cared when I told them I'm gay. This is about *us*. You like big!" Tomas thrust his arms out, wildly. "You like being the center of attention—everyone's attention—really in their face. I'm not like that."

"In their face." Nico blinked back the burn in his eyes.

He should be used to this by now.

It was always the same. Nico was too much. Too touchy-feely. Too colorful.

Too fucking loud.

He formed a plastic smile. Never mind that behind it he felt achingly empty and inadequate. He wouldn't let Tomas know how shattering his words were. How much he'd hoped this time would be different.

When would Nico learn it was pointless to hope?

"I'm truly sorry you feel this way," Nico said. "You don't need to say anything else. I won't make a scene. My big boy pants are on."

Nico turned his back on Tomas and Pi Zeta-fucking-Eta and stalked off.

Harrison campus blurred as he cut through it. In the middle of the brightly lit corridor leading to the central library, Nico's phone vibrated.

Elisa: C'mon, Nico. Call me! This is a disaster.

Not the best timing, but maybe her problems would help him forget his own. He hit dial and braced for it.

"Nico! Thank God. I'm so screwed. The wedding planner quit today. Her mother is sick and she needs to go to Boston to take care of her. I can't believe this. How can this be happening? The wedding's in three months and—"

"I'll take over, Elisa."

"What?"

"I'll take over and make sure everything's perfect."

"Oh my God, Nico, you're the best."

Nico raised an eyebrow. Clearly this was what she'd wanted him to say. "It's what little brothers do."

"Wait, you were supposed to be in New York. With your boyfriend."

"Ex-boyfriend."

"But . . ."

"Just happened."

"Oh, boo. I'm so sorry to be dumping on you now."

Great choice of words. "You're not. This is perfect. I don't want to go home, and you need someone in Philly to make sure your wedding is amazing."

"Are you sure? I could always look around for someone else . . ."

He snorted softly. They both knew she'd never find anyone decent at this late date. All the best planners were booked.

"I got this, E. Just pay for me to stay in Philly and give me some spending money, and I'll make sure this is everything you dreamed of." And that Nico wanted, but would never have.

"Boo, you are the best. I'll make sure Papà pays you what he was going to give the planner. You'll be all set up."

Nico scoffed. "No way Papà will pay me the same as your planner."

"If he doesn't want to hear me whine every day, he will."

A laugh barked from his throat. Their father hadn't been able to refuse Elisa ever since she learned how to talk. "Whatever you say."

"Thank you, thank you, thank you! You're the best brother ever! Sorry about that douche canoe."

"Let it go, E. He's not worth it." He really wasn't, and Nico wanted to bury the hurt that came from his rejection. "I'll find a place and send you the deets to pass on to Papà so he can cut the check."

"I love you to the moon and back."

"A hundred million googolplex times." Nico smiled at their traditional signoff. Something they'd been doing since they were in kindergarten. "I'll call you tomorrow. And E?"

"Yeah?"

"Don't tell anyone Tomas and I broke up. I'm not in the mood for the barrage of calls."

"You got it."

He hit end and stared at the phone. Philly was unexpected, but at least it would give him time to rethink his life.

Luke

Kent: I'm sorry, Luke, but I've met someone who lives closer to me and I want to be with them. It's better for both of us. Long distance wasn't working.

LUCAS "LUKE" DeRosa stared at the laptop, stunned. An email? Nine months together, and Kent broke up in an *email*?

The cowardly, cheating bastard!

This couldn't be happening. Luke had bummed rides and taken the bus to spend weekends together. He'd almost failed a midterm because he spent the weekend before nursing Kent when he'd been sick. Hell, Luke had planned his entire summer around Kent. Gave up the job back home to go to Philly and intern at the same accounting firm. They were going to *live* together.

Oh, *fuck*. Their apartment.

His dorm room door opened, and his roommate sauntered in like he'd never had a bad day in his life. Luke glanced up, and Coury's smile vanished.

"Yo, what's wrong, bro?" He plopped next to Luke on the bed. "You don't look good. What happened?"

"Kent broke up with me."

"What?" Coury straightened. "Why?"

That was what Luke wanted to know. "Said the distance thing was too much, and he met someone else."

"What a fucker. Seriously?"

God, he wished it was a joke. "Shiiiiit. I sublet the apartment for us both and he's staying with his new—with this other guy now."

He should have seen the signs. Kent had blamed Luke for their inability to connect. Said Luke's baseball schedule kept them apart. And being the fool he was, Luke accepted it had been his fault. Made up excuses to believe him when Kent said he couldn't drive to Harrison.

"I'm so fucking stupid."

Coury put a casual arm around his roommate. "Don't blame yourself for his assholery."

"Assholery?" Luke snorted. "Is that a real word?"

"Ninety-nine percent sure it is. This isn't on you."

"Yeah, up here I get it." He tapped his head before moving his hand down to his chest. "But here?"

"I'm sorry, Luke." Coury clapped Luke across the back. "Don't sweat Philly. We'll figure something out."

Luke laughed. "I didn't know you were coming too. Though help with rent would be ace."

"You know what I mean." Coury got up and pulled his laptop from his backpack. "The campus has a roommate-wanted site. That's how I found the off-campus place I'm living in this summer. Don't know if I saw any listings in Philly, but I remember seeing people advertise for other cities."

So many problems with that idea. "Did I mention it's a one-bedroom apartment?"

"Details." Coury typed. "First thing is to find you a roommate, *then* you can worry about who's sleeping where."

"You don't need to do this. I'll figure it out."

"I'm sure you will, but I know you. You'll go into a funk and procrastinate. You've only got a couple of weeks to sort this out."

"Right, because *so* many people at Harrison are going to Philly for the summer and still need a place to live."

"Hey, things happen." Coury nodded pointedly at Luke. "People get dumped. I'm sure there are more than a few people who've had a change of plans."

"Sure. Tons."

"All you need is one." He spun the screen around. "Fill out the details."

Luke stared blankly. His choices were limited. If he had to pay for the apartment by himself, he'd need to get a part-time job over the summer *and* during the school year. Both of those would affect his job prospects after he graduated.

Asking his family was a no-go, too.

"Right." Luke took the laptop and started typing. "All I need is one."

CHAPTER TWO

Nico

Nico glared at his phone screen as he hurried toward his sociology lecture. Elisa smiled sheepishly, her cheeks ruddy, her hair a mass of almost black curls around her shoulders.

"Seriously, E. Papà's paying me half what he was paying the wedding planner. Half. Have you seen what rents cost? There won't be enough to eat and go out."

"Go out . . ." He could hear her eyes roll. "You have savings. Or you could room with someone?"

Nico cast his head toward the cloudy sky. Okay, so yes, he had money. But that was *not* the point. He didn't want this job to cost him.

As for rooming . . . his stomach twisted sharply. He had it good with Isaiah at Harrison, but a roommate like him was one in a million. Not everyone could handle Nicodemo Giacomo Amato.

He'd be in for an awkward summer.

Lips pressed in a firm line, he met Elisa's pleading brown eyes. His jaw unlocked. Elisa was doing that thing. That weaseling into his heart thing. That thing Nico couldn't get grumpy at. "Fine," he sighed dramatically. "I'll share with someone or I'll tap my savings. But if Papà starts getting fussy and ultra-demanding, you gotta rein him in with those puppy eyes."

She snorted, rolling her eyes. "He's not that bad."

"Sister, please." He snapped his fingers dramatically, hitting a passerby in the face.

A little overzealous. His bad. "Oh, my. I'm sorry," Nico said, eyes latching on to the guy's disapproving frown.

"Whatever."

Don't check him out. Don't.

But Nico did. He couldn't help it. Because the guy was quite the specimen of athletic grace. Lean and toned and very, very hot. Brown floppy hair and hazel eyes. Dark shirt. Navy jeans. Big hands. Bigger feet . . .

Nico jerked his head up and pressed his fingers against his chest. "Sincerely sorry. You know, about your face."

Hottie remained a beat, hesitating, frown deepening as his gaze sized him up.

Nico pushed the pain of that judgement under all the other such moments he'd experienced in his life. Just another Tuesday.

Nico stepped to Hottie's right, and Hottie lurched to Nico's left. They collided, Nico's foot stomping on Hottie's toes. For crying out loud.

They both corrected, and it became a ridiculous mirrored dance.

Heat whispered up Nico's neck, and someone giggled. His traitorous sister, who still stared at him from the phone he clutched.

Nico stopped moving, turned sideways and swept his arms theatrically to the side. "After you."

Hottie passed like he was on fire, tossing out a sarcastic, "Thanks."

Nico admired the magnificent ass as it moved down the sidewalk. Too bad he was an asshole. "Stupid fucker."

The guy's step stuttered. His shoulders lifted in a deep inhale, then he kept walking. His "Fuck my life so hard" trailed on a breeze toward Nico.

Fuck *his* life? Poor hottie had a run-in with a bit of flamboyance. His life was ruined. He'd have to hide it from his jock friends. He'd be depressed for the whole day.

Nico kissed a middle finger at his retreating figure and swallowed to fill the achy inferiority in his gut. The loneliness.

"Boo?" Elisa's voice sounded far away. Nico returned his focus to her. "You okay?"

"Fine, E. Tell Papà I'll call him tonight with an update. And don't worry. I'll find a place to stay."

"You're the best!"

Yeah, the best drama queen.

Luke

LUKE LAY IN BED, awake, unable to switch off his mind.

Completely screwed might sum up his situation.

He was due to leave for Philly in a week, and the only response to his *roommate wanted* ad had been from a dodgy-as-fuck sugar daddy. Being asked what he was willing to do for financial help turned Luke's guts inside out.

This couldn't be his only option, surely.

It wouldn't be.

If it came to it, he'd get a second job. Realistically, he would manage that. Scrape by.

Ideally, though, he wouldn't. There were social events as part of his unpaid internship, and attending them was more important than the work. Or so his father had claimed as he added more money than they'd discussed to Luke's account.

"Thousands of people have great GPAs. They want to find out if you fit with everyone else who works there."

Fuck. He needed to find a roommate. 'Acceptable' might not matter.

Luke groaned, sat up, and quietly retrieved his phone, not wanting to wake Coury. It was close to one, and both their alarms went off at seven.

He unlocked his phone, and the screen blinded him. Quickly, he dulled the brightness and checked his messages. Nothing.

So much for the online bulletin board.

He rubbed the end of his phone against his forehead. Fuuuck.

Vibrations racing over his skin had Luke jerking his phone down. A new message had popped into his inbox.

His heart raced as he caught the forwarding details from the bulletin board. The subject read: Room in Philly still available?

Okay, Luke didn't believe in fate and all that bullcrap, but. Great fucking timing.

He read over the message. A student named Nico from Harrison. A last-minute summer change; he needed a room in Philly. No weird sugar daddy vibes, thank God.

Luke hurriedly logged in to the bulletin board and replied.

Hey Nico,

Yes, still looking for a roommate.

Apartment is in a good location close to downtown. A cozy place with a nice kitchen, decent bath and shower, too. Really lovely landlord. You saw the link with photos?

Luke

Luke jammed a pillow between his back and the wall and stared at his phone, hoping this Nico guy was still up. That he'd answer—

Luke grinned at another vibration.

Hi Luke,

Saw the pictures. Looks like a decent place. There's only one picture of the master room though. And just writing this, I suddenly realize why you used the term "cozy." It's a one-bedder isn't it?

You seem all right. (You've got grammar going for you) And you're a guy, so you've hit a major button there. But sharing a bed might be jumping the gun a little. ;-)

Sorry, will have to pass.

Good luck,
Nico

Hey Nico,

Don't pass, please? That "king" bed is really two twins connected by a bed bridge. I swear it's two beds, we can push them apart. Please, I need a roommate who doesn't expect me to pay him back in favors. (Don't ask. Okay, do: there are some very cocky men out there. Pun intended. I mean, yes, I'm gay, but no, that doesn't mean I'll jump anyone. One, I like to know a guy first. And two, I've just been royally screwed by my cheating ex).

What I am trying to say is: you need a place. I have one. I'm sure we can figure out acceptable sleeping arrangements.

Luke

Luke,

Sorry about your cheating ex. I guess he's the reason you're stuck looking for a roommate? What a bastard. I say this with confidence, because I've dated a bastard or two or three in my lifetime. (Sixteen, to be precise). So take my word on it, leaving you with all the rent is a sucky move.

Nico

Nico,

Does that mean you'll take the place? Or was that a gentle letdown? I can't tell.

(Please take the place.)

L.

Luke,

Honestly, I wasn't sure when I sent it either. My sympathetic side says ***take it, you idiot.***

My logical side says ***one room? A whole summer? What if we're not compatible?***

Nico,

What are you concerned about? Let me assure you, I am not a pervert.

Luke,

Truth? Guys don't often like what they see. I make them uncomfortable. I need to know you are secure in your own masculinity. That you won't care.

Okay, so maybe I'm being worried for nothing, but I banged into a guy today who looked at me like filth. I'm sick of it.

Rooming makes me nervous. But I suppose, like you, I'm kinda desperate for a place.

Nico,

Okay, that guy sounds like a dick.

If you're anything like your emails, I'm sure we'll make it through three months. But, if it makes you feel better, you can ask me questions to feel out our compatibility.

Totally not grinning that you're desperate for a place,

L.

Luke,

I revealed my hand too soon, I see.

Below is my phone number. This email business is getting tedious. Text me.

Luke plugged Nico's number into his phone, grinning in the dark like a hopeful idiot.

Luke: Ask away.

CHAPTER THREE

Nico

Luke: Can you really arrange a wedding?

Nico: My sister thinks so.

Luke: lol.

Nico: Seriously, she's my best friend. My summer plans blew up, so I'll make it happen for her

Nico: Or go down swinging.

Luke: That's awesome. And what happens if you go down swinging?

Nico: I bought tickets to Siberia. She hates the cold. She'll never come looking for me.

Luke: Winnipeg might be safer. Russia doesn't like gays.

Nico: True, hadn't thought of that.

Luke: Maybe you need me to be your planner.

Nico snorted as the door to his dorm opened and his roomie, Isaiah, waltzed in.

Nico: Only if you flee to Canada with me.

Dark, long-haired Isaiah plopped onto Nico's bed, smelling like he'd had an extended yoga session. Or indulged in marathon sex. "Go shower, pretty."

"Who are you texting, smiling like you put Icy Hot in Tomas's underwear?" Isaiah lunged for Nico's phone.

Nico snatched it away, shielding the screen. "Child, didn't your nonna teach you it's not polite to read your friend's phone when he's flirtexting?"

"Flirtexting?" Isaiah's eyebrows rocketed. "Is that foreplay before sexting?"

"Pfft." Nico flicked his hand in front of his face. "Is that what you and Darren do when he's away?"

"Oh no, you're not turning this on me." Isaiah pulled out his hair tie, and thick locks fell to his shoulders. "*You* said you were flirtexting, not me."

"Yes, well, that isn't *real* flirting. Just being silly." Nico peeled off his T-shirt and shrugged into a black satin button-down.

"Not flirting, but you're wearing *that* to meet the guy?"

"I need to make a good impression. He's interning at the accounting firm of Stuffy & Staid, which means he's smart and cultured."

"Of course. No one at Stuffy & Staid would be anything else."

"Your Mr. Downer Pants attitude is noted." Nico refused to let it spoil his mood. "Luke sounds like a nice guy. He's funny—"

"In his texts."

"—smart, and plays baseball for Harrison. What could be more yummy?"

"You're thinking of rooming with a jock? *You*? Mr. Go Hard or Buy Viagra?"

"That would be a problem if we were living on campus and he was playing." He checked his outfit in the mirror. "It's half-season now. None of his friends will be dropping in."

Isaiah rolled off Nico's bed. "First, it's off-season, not half-season."

"Look at you, dating Harrison's star soccer player and up on all the lingo." He stuck out his tongue at Isaiah before fixing his belt.

"I'd take offense at that, but Darren *is* the star of the team. I can't embarrass him by being ignorant."

"As if. That boy worships you." Why couldn't Nico find someone like that? Who looked at him like he was everything? Who looked at him and didn't want to change a single thing?

"I'm just saying, you answered an ad for a roommate, not a boyfriend."

"I get it. But a) it doesn't hurt to look nice and b) there's nothing wrong with having a hot roommate. Being with me seems to have done you some good, no?"

Isaiah snorted and shook his head. "So wrong."

"Seriously, 'Saiah. You know me. I won't jump the guy or ask if I can put my tongue down his throat to see if we're a match."

"Fair enough. But maybe be a bit nicer to him. The first time we met, you told me I needed a haircut."

"Yes, I did." He winked as he opened the door. "And you still do."

Luke

Landlord: Yes, I can do a second lease once you find a roommate. Good luck with it. And sorry your original roommate didn't work out.

Luke: Thanks so much. This is really a big help.

HOPEFULLY NICO in person was as cool as virtual Nico.

"That the lady you're renting from?" Coury never looked up from his video game.

"Yeah, she's pretty cool. She'll do a second contract if I find someone."

"*When* you find someone. Think positive."

"I'm trying, but people aren't beating down the door to spend the summer in Philadelphia." How big a fool was he, turning down spots in Boston, Chicago, and D.C. so he could spend the summer with Kent?

"Hey now, don't be dissin' on the City of Boy-on-Boy Love."

Luke smiled until he remembered Coury first used that when he learned Luke and Kent were sharing a one-bedroom this summer. "There will be none of that this summer for me. I'm only looking for a roommate. And, I may have found one. Maybe."

"Maybe? What's wrong with this Nero guy?"

"Nico. At least that's what he says his name is."

"You don't believe him?"

Luke shut the laptop screen. "I searched social media for him and came up empty."

"Lots of people don't use their name for social media." Coury shrugged. "Future employers don't need to see me drunk in a toga or flipping off the camera."

"There is that, but what if this is Kent or one of his stupid friends trying to catfish me?"

Luke didn't think that was the case. At least, he certainly hoped not.

"That's always possible." Coury set the laptop down. "What's also possible is this guy who has you smiling at your phone as you text and laughing when you read his, who's helping out his sister because *his* boyfriend dumped him too, is legit. In which case, you're going to spend the summer with another funny, smart, normal guy from Harrison. The only differences are he won't be as incredibly good-looking as your current roommate, and he'll be gay."

"You're practically gay, so not much change there."

"Don't be hating on the bi guy just because he's dating a girl and off the gay-boy menu."

Luke laughed. "No hate here. I get the best of both worlds. We can talk about hot guys and you get it, but I don't have to worry that you'll try to steal them away."

"Hmm. Maybe I should dump Hailey. Then we could do a 'let's pick a hot guy and see which one of us gets him' experiment." He got off the bed and spread his arms. "I'm sure I'd win. Not many can resist all this."

Luke picked up a hand towel from the floor and threw it at Coury. Perfect strike to the face. "Of course. Just like you were sure you'd win the 'who can get the better grades this year' bet."

"Which, my incredibly good-looking, super smart, amazingly nice roommate, is why you are also socially awkward. That was sarcasm. I've never beaten you at anything . . . yet."

Clearly, Luke wasn't any of those things to Kent. "Sorry. You might want to add ginormous dumb-ass to the list."

"Nah, I'd never kick my best friend when he's down." He handed Luke the towel. "Nice throw."

"It's one of my few good qualities. Right up there with striking out when it comes to men."

"Stop." He grabbed Luke by the shoulders and stared until he looked up. "Kent was a fucking twat-waffle. First time I met him, he struck me as a total poser. I probably should have said something, but figured if I did, it would drive a wedge between us."

"Probably. Then I'd come slinking back asking you to forgive me."

"Which would never be an issue." He smiled and pulled Luke into a headlock. The hold turned into a hug before they moved apart. "My point is, you're way too good for him. Yep, that is totally a line you tell folks when they're hurting from a break-up, but seriously? It's true. Forget looks or money or even . . . shudder . . . *baseball*, you are a super nice guy. The best. This really, truly is Kent's loss."

"You didn't see the super-rich, hot guy he's dating now."

"I bet you anything they don't last the summer."

"Anything?" Luke leered at his friend.

"Well, I ain't gonna sleep with you."

"Ewww. Brain bleach."

Coury barked out a laugh. "Whatever. Don't be so literal. I'm just saying, you're not the loser here, he is. And karma is gonna kick him in the nuts."

"Square?"

"Exactly, square in the nuts."

Luke's phone buzzed. "I have to go meet Nico. Wish me luck."

Lots of luck.

Nico

Luke: Here. Got a table to the right of the door.

Luke: Your right that is.

Nico: Wow! Someone's eager.

Luke: Would it bruise your ego if I said I'm usually early?

Nico: Yes. Totally.

Luke: You were right, I'm eager.

NICO LAUGHED as he pushed his phone into his pocket. An anxious chuckle leaked out of him, and he slowed his step toward the café. God, he hoped they hit it off in real life as much as they did virtually.

He paused a few paces from the door and swept a hand through his hair. He tugged his shirt and smoothed his hands over his ass. Yep, he was looking good.

Powered by nervous energy, he yanked open the door.

More than a few heads jerked in his direction. He slicked on a flirty grin and scanned the tables to his right—

His stomach dropped.

Oh, *hell* no. Please, please don't be Luke.

Sitting to the right, in shorts, T-shirt, baseball cap, and flip-flops, looking expectantly at the door, was the guy he'd accidentally face-punched.

Nico frantically looked at the tables behind him, next to him. All had two or more people, chatting away. No one else looked like they were waiting for someone.

He glanced at Luke again, to find Luke's equally shocked gaze rooted to him.

Well, fuck his life.

Luke's eyes raked over him from head to foot, and Nico's stomach dropped heavily to his feet. It took him more energy than usual to plaster on a fake smile.

The disappointment cut.

He searched Luke's unfairly hot face, hoping at least for a bruise from where Nico had struck him. Nothing. Just a well-defined jaw, sharp nose, and a cap over brown hair. Obviously a jock. Obviously not going to work out.

The vibration on his wrist wrenched his gaze from Luke. Incoming.

Elisa: How'd the meet and greet go? You set?

Yeah, things were set—set up to be a train wreck in slow motion. Still, he couldn't just walk out—Luke had clearly seen him, and while Luke might be a judgmental asshole, Nico wasn't a dick.

His feet felt like concrete as he moved.

Luke blew out a breath. Yeah, he got how fucked-up this was too.

Another buzz.

Elisa: I need details. Papà's driving me nuts.

"Girl." The word hissed from between his teeth.

"What?"

Nico tore his eyes off the message. He'd made it to the table, and Luke was frowning at him. Fuck.

"Sorry. That was for my sister." He held up the phone and winced. "She's asking for minute-by-minute updates."

Luke sank back in his seat. "Thought you were . . ."

"Calling you a girl?" Nico snorted. "Yeah, no. At least not on the first date."

His joke landed like an anvil, and Luke stiffened.

"That's a joke." Nico swallowed a sigh. "The more nervous I am, the worse they get."

Awkward tension tugged at Nico's stomach. They'd chatted so easily online; he'd expected—*hoped for*—smooth sailing.

Luke rubbed his nape, looking like he wanted to say something, but couldn't for the life of him find words.

Nico tapped his fingers over the tabletop and addressed the elephant in the room. "About the other day. I'd been freshly dumped. It was a shitty day. Sorry about the face punching."

A smile smoothed the lines on Luke's brow. The first smile Nico had ever seen on the guy. The corners of Luke's lips twitched, and his brown eyes sparkled warmly. The intensity of it was enough to make Nico shiver.

"Not to sound all competitive," Luke said, voice creamy and deep, "but that was the day *my* ex dumped me . . . in an email."

"An *email*?"

"I was taking a walk after reading it. A grumpy stomp, if we're being accurate."

Nico raised his hands. "You win the shittiest day contest."

"An award I could've lived without."

"Don't try to pawn it off on me. I win it often enough."

They laughed, and some of the awkwardness dissipated. Not enough that Nico forgot the look Luke had given him when they first met, but enough to settle into the conversation.

Luke regarded Nico, eyes roaming his face. Nico shivered under it, battling the wave of inferiority that rushed up his chest. So what if Luke didn't like what he saw?

They were there about a room, not anything else.

Luke's gaze narrowed on Nico's lips, and Nico wished he could rewind that afternoon on the phone with Elisa. Wished he hadn't been quite so dramatic. Wished he'd said something that Luke might have grinned at . . .

Nico glanced away from him, struggling to keep the emotion off his face. The disappointment.

"Can we start this over?" Luke held out his hand. "Lucas DeRosa. Luke."

Nico swallowed. "Nico Amato . . . Nicodemo really, but *please*, do not call me that. My mother uses it when she's mad."

Another smile.

Fuck, those were going to be problematic.

"Sure. I'll stick with Nico." Luke removed the Harrison Baseball cap and ran his hand up and down the back of his head. "So this roommate thing . . ."

"Yeah . . ."

"Here's the thing, I *really* need a roommate this summer and you were . . . *are* the only one who responded that could possibly work. Do you want to talk or do we pick up our bat and ball and go home?"

Instinct told Nico to take the opening Luke gave him and leave. They'd gone from sure they were compatible to "might possibly work" in three minutes. If he signed the lease, they'd be stuck together all summer.

Could he really blame their rocky in-person start on them both having craptastic days right before they met?

Nico wanted to, but was that his dick talking?

A pulsation from his watch reminded him he needed to answer Elisa. He gnawed his lip and threw himself in the fire. "Yeah, okay. Let's give this a shot."

CHAPTER FOUR

Nico

Nico stared at the lit-up Pi Zeta Eta house. Music and the booming chant of a couple dozen jocks made the path vibrate. Isaiah squished his nose in distaste, and Nico was almost sorry he'd dragged him here. Almost.

Nico had insisted Isaiah come along, laughing that it'd be shits and giggles. Just a quick mission in and out to retrieve his portable charger. Tomas knew he was coming for it.

Really, Nico had towed him there for moral support, because looking at the monster frat house reminded Nico of his place. Or better said, reminded him where his place wasn't.

Jocks didn't like him. Didn't get him. Never would.

"You sure this is a good idea?" Isaiah asked warily.

"If I don't get it back today, he'll need to send it to me. Which I know he'd never do. So."

"Yeah, but it's just a portable charger."

"I paid over a hundred dollars for it."

"Right, but you barely used it before you loaned it to Tomas. Why the burning need to get it back now?"

"I loaned it to him when we were together. Me and my stuff are a package deal. You don't get to keep my things if you break up with me."

"So, it's the principle."

That sounded better than because he'd seen Tomas laughing with his mates at the cafeteria and had the petty urge to wipe at least half the smirk off his face. Seriously, why did Nico have to be the only one who felt like shit? "Exactly."

"Are you sure about this?"

Was he? Probably not, but . . . "He didn't want me, 'Saiah."

Isaiah sighed. "Yeah, yeah, I get it. Let's get your charger back so you can move on."

They approached the door and the frat dudes vaping beside it. Nico's step slowed, nervousness swirling in his stomach as they entered.

Nico scanned the common area. Isaiah elbowed him and pointed toward the kitchen. "He's there."

And there Tomas was. In the narrow hallway, leaned back against the wall, ubiquitous red plastic cup in hand. He was chatting with a tall, blond preppy guy, their smiles more than frat-brotherly.

Tomas laughed, chin lifting, and his gaze snagged onto Nico. His smile faded.

Nico straightened, held his head high, and strode over. "Do you have it?"

Terse and rude, but it fit his mood. Tomas couldn't wait fifteen minutes to start flirting?

"It's on my desk." He shooed Nico toward Isaiah. "I'll get it in a minute."

"Oh, heavens no, dear. I wouldn't want you to exert yourself. I know the way." Before Tomas could answer, he herded Isaiah toward the stairs.

"You dated *him*?" Tomas's preppy guy asked, derision dripping from his voice.

"*He* thought we were dating," Tomas said. "But you know me. I don't go for guys like that."

A snigger. "Yeah, I couldn't see it."

Nico clenched his jaw to keep from shouting *you went for me well enough when my cock was in your ass.*

He felt Isaiah's hand on his lower back. "Stick to the plan."

"Right." Nico tore his gaze from the hall and led them to Tomas's room.

As promised, the charger sat in plain view on the desk. Snatching it wasn't as satisfying at Nico had hoped.

Fighting back tears, he scooped up a black Sharpie from the desk, walked over to Tomas's bed, spun the pillow around, and uncapped the marker.

"Nico!" Isaiah hissed from the doorway, glancing left and right. "What are you doing?"

"Closure."

"Closure?"

Nico scrawled, *We dated! Fucker!* on the white background. He underlined the last word three times, capped the pen, and tossed it on the bed. "Now, we can go."

I DON'T GO for guys like that.

That summed up his entire dating life.

No matter how great he was in bed, no matter how much he cared, all guys judged him for his campy outbursts.

He was sick of it.

Nico dashed a hand over his burning eyes and bowed deeper into his closet to avoid Isaiah spotting him.

He'd had a night to get over the moment with Tomas yesterday, he should be fine by now. Should've pushed it aside . . .

Nico fingered the sleeve of his slim-fit mulberry velvet jacket.

Rubbed the stretchy tapered pants that looked fantastic with his Berluti shoes.

Was it over the top?

Maybe pride kept him from listening to the truth. He was too much.

If he toned it down, just a bit, acted more like the everyday man . . . maybe he'd have more luck. In life, and in love.

Nico shut the closet and grabbed his car keys. He had a wardrobe to update.

Nico: Packed. OMW.

Luke: I'm ready. Game sucks. We're losing.

Nico: There's always a next game.

NICO'S PHONE bounced in his pocket as he hopped up the steps.

Why did guys like cargo shorts so much? Maybe he shouldn't have put so much stuff in his pockets. But what was the point of having them if you didn't use them?

Ugh, he'd never felt so uncomfortable and bulky.

A cheer erupted from the house, and someone shouted, "Go!"

Nico knocked, but no one heard him over the noise. The door opened with a testing push, and he poked his head inside. An odd assortment of gym bags, a suitcase, and a suit carrier sat inside the otherwise empty foyer.

He entered and shut the door, hard enough to say "hello." As if on cue, Luke appeared in casual shorts and a loose T-shirt.

His eyes shone with a smile the moment he saw Nico, and Nico reined in the desire to toss out a flirty hello. He settled on a small dude-like grin with an accompanying half-nod to match his appearance.

Luke gestured Nico to join him in the living room. "Can we finish watching the game? It's bottom of the ninth and the Phillies are rallying against the Nats."

"Umm . . . okay, but I think I'm illegally parked."

"Don't worry. Campus cops don't bother anyone unless we call. Besides, this shouldn't take long."

Luke's gaze roamed over Nico's attire, and his brow quivered.

The look was better than the one Luke had cast him that first day. This look was baffled, surprised, and definitely curious.

Nico would take it.

He followed Luke inside the living area to the back of a couch seating three other guys. Guys who looked like they'd either just gotten up, been drinking since noon, or some combination of both.

The batter got a hit, and Luke and his friends started shouting at the players on base to run. A coach was waving his arms wildly, and the player rounded the bag and sped past.

"Oh, shit!" someone shouted. "It's gonna be close!"

The catcher got the ball on one hop, and the base runner plowed into him. When the umpire made a punching motion with his right hand, Luke and the others groaned.

"Son of a bitch, Soto's got a cannon!" Luke said.

"Fuckin' right. I can't believe he threw out Segura."

"Did your team lose?" Nico asked, stepping up to Luke, trying to sound interested.

Luke shook his head. "Segura was the winning run. It's tied."

"So is it going to overtime?"

"Extra innings, yeah." Luke glanced toward a lazily grinning guy with sinfully toned arms on his other side. "Nico, this is my roommate and best friend, Coury."

Coury scanned Nico and held out his hand. "Nice to finally meet you. You're a life saver for Luke after the dickwad who-shall-not-be-named screwed him over."

"This works out well for me after the douchenozzle who-shall-not-be-named fucked *me* over."

Coury snorted and smacked Luke approvingly on the back. "Luke told me. Sorry to hear it."

"It's old news." Nico nodded toward the television. "Did you want to stay and watch the end?"

"You don't mind?" Luke's eyes sparked with gratitude—and who the hell could say no to that.

"We don't have a schedule to keep." Nico fished his keys out of his pocket. "Let me move my car while they do the coin toss thingy."

"Coin toss?" Coury asked with a baffled frown.

Nico winced. "To see who goes first in extra innings?"

The two guys Nico hadn't met snickered. That sounded about right.

Luke guided Nico toward the door, a soft grin twitching his lips. He spoke low. "They don't do a coin toss in baseball. That's football. The away team hits in the top of the inning and the home team gets last ups."

Nico's face burned, and he cast his gaze to the floorboards. "Right. Sorry."

"Don't sweat it." Luke gently shoulder-nudged him into the foyer. "Let me put my stuff in your car, and we can come in and watch the end of the game. If it drags, we'll leave."

Nico swallowed. "Sure."

Luke's gaze scrolled over Nico's face, and he hefted his bags over his shoulder. "Know what? Let's just leave."

Luke

Coury: Bottom 14th. Glad we don't need a coin toss after each inning.

Luke: Don't be a douche. Nico's cool. Tom and Miles were dicks to laugh.

Coury: Yeah, but it was funny.

Luke: No. It wasn't.

LUKE PUSHED his phone into his pocket. "Good thing we left. Game's still going."

"Did you want to listen to it? I'm pretty sure the satellite radio gets all the games."

"Thanks, but I doubt you're interested." Luke avoided looking over. "We can listen to whatever you like."

"What gave away my lack of baseball acumen? Overtime or the coin toss?" Nico snuck a glance at Luke and made a self-deprecating face.

"Both?" Luke grinned. "It's all good. I guess that makes you a football fan."

"Only if you mean English football." Nico tapped a button and the radio came to life. "Ask me about soccer and I'm good. Everything else? I'm only there to stare at the hot guys."

"Did you play?" Luke raked his eyes over Nico's body, reading it like it might give him the answer.

Nico wore shorts, revealing toned legs, and a T-shirt that showed off a tapered body. He clearly worked out somehow.

His dark hair was neatly styled—the only thing about his appearance that resembled the Nico he'd met twice before. It looked good on him, swept back. Gave his big brown eyes more room to show off—damn, he had nice ones.

Nico caught him looking and shifted. "Pretty much played since I could walk. Papà played in college and then in a men's league in Brooklyn. When my older brother was born, he coached. He's a referee now. My nonno—grandfather—refereed for forty years—and I'm babbling."

Luke laughed. "I think it's cool your family is so into soccer. How come you don't play for Harrison?"

Nico returned his gaze to the road, voice quieter. Sadder. "My teammates in high school made it clear they didn't want a fag on the team, so I stopped playing."

The fuck? "They got away with that?" Luke gritted his teeth. Sometimes he hated the world. "If you don't want to talk about it, I get it. I can't believe the school let them do that. Harrison wouldn't."

Which was a good thing for Luke. He loved baseball.

"I never told anyone at the school," Nico said softly. "I just quit after coming out. Like they wanted."

Luke swallowed. "Sorry coming out cost you something you loved, but I admire your courage. I wasn't secure enough to come out until after I graduated."

Nico's grip on the steering wheel made the leather creak. "Elisa, my sister, wanted me to report it to the school, but that would've been pointless."

"Really? Your school didn't have a no-discrimination policy?"

"They did, but . . . well, you know. There's one set of rules for most of us, and one for those whose parents have ginormous bank accounts."

Luke nodded. Harrison had some of that. "So you're one of the have-nots, like me."

"I guess. I mean, my family is well off, but nothing close to qualifying for the unwritten rules."

"Sorry. Again."

"Yeah, me too. Mostly because I should have said fuck it and pushed back. Like Isaiah did."

"Your roommate? What'd he do?"

A smile softened Nico's face. "He fought back. Harrison was going to give the Gage Scholar award to Darren Gage, whose great-something-grandfather founded the school and the program. Isaiah filed a grievance and it was granted."

"Did he get the scholarship?"

"He got something, alright." Nico laughed.

Luke liked amused Nico more than the angsty version. "You're totally gonna need to explain that."

Nico gave Luke a wonderfully detailed retelling of Isaiah's story. Which turned out to be quite the romance. ". . . they're so sweetly in love I might get diabetes just from sharing their story with you."

"Might get it from hearing it, too."

Nico glanced at Luke, those brown eyes skating over his face, and Luke squirmed. Did Nico hear the jealousy in his voice? Could he see how hurt he still was over Kent? Could he see how much Luke wanted to rewind the last six months and do things differently? Figure out where he went wrong?

Luke rubbed his nape, and Nico's smile dissipated. "I love their story, but it makes me wish I'd made better decisions. I'm working on not making that mistake again."

"Amen!" Luke pumped up his hands, startling Nico into a laugh.

"Oh, lord help me." Nico snapped a hand over his heart. "What about you? No coming out horror stories?"

"Iowa isn't the worst place for gay rights. I mean, we were one of the first to approve gay marriage, but I didn't have confidence it would go well. Especially with my teammates."

"Yep." Nico pointed to himself. "Living proof that teammates can suck. So when did you come out?"

"Told my parents after I graduated, Coury first day on campus—he was my roommate—and the team just before spring training started."

"How'd that go?"

"Better than I expected. We had workouts all fall semester, and Coury and I both figured Dustin, the team captain, wouldn't freak out, so I told him. As we expected, he was cool about it. He even helped me come out to the rest of the team."

"He told them?"

Luke snorted. "No, that's a chickenshit way to do it. At our first team meeting, he had everyone tell the others something personal. Mine was to tell them I was gay."

"Holy Mary, Mother of God! I'd have passed out if I had to do that."

"Yeah, I almost puked waiting for my turn." Two years later, it still made him sweat. "Then I blurted out, 'I'm gay' when they got to me. Dustin asked if anyone had a problem with it. No one said anything. Having his support really made a difference."

"Dustin sounds like a great guy."

"He is." Luke's phone vibrated and he pulled it out. "Coury must be giving me an update."

"Seriously, we can listen to the game it you like."

"Maybe, let me see if it's still—" Oh. Not from Coury.

"Still what?" Nico looked over. "I take it that's not about the game."

"Um . . . no. Facebook update from my ex."

"Ah."

"Yeah." He should have put the phone away, but he couldn't stop himself from looking. Pictures of the happy couple on the new boyfriend's yacht. *Blowing off steam before I have to knuckle down and work this summer. Thank you, Sebastian, for an amazing time.*

Right. Amazing. Not boring, like Luke.

"You should block him and be done with it."

"Huh?" Should he?

"Been there, done that. It never ends well." Nico shook his head. "Like I said, block him."

"But we're still friends." They were. "And we have to work together this summer."

They did.

"Honey, he sounds like a player. They're never worth the time."

Luke frowned at Nico. "You don't even know him."

"You're right." Nico kept his gaze on the road. "I shouldn't have said that."

Neither should Luke have been so sharp. "Sorry, I didn't mean to bark at you."

"It's okay. I was out of line."

Staring at the photos, maybe *he* was the one who didn't know Kent. "No, you weren't. It's still a bit raw."

And it touched a bit too close to home. Kent had called him boring once, during an argument. Said he wanted more excitement in their relationship.

He clicked off the phone, stuffed it in his bag, and fell back against the seat. "Not gonna look anymore. If you see me checking out his timeline, smack me and take my phone."

"Oh my, the things you say."

"I'm serious. He's moved on, and I should too." He sucked in a deep breath and exhaled loudly. "How about we listen to the end of the game?"

Nico

WHOEVER THOUGHT to build rest stops on the Pennsylvania Turnpike deserved a fucking medal. Or at least a good blow job. Not that Nico would volunteer to make payment.

As a kid, Nico's parents always reminded him to use the bathroom before the start of a trip. Without Mom to keep him on point, he forgot to go before he left to pick up Luke. Some days, adulting was harder than others.

Nico stretched to work out the kinks in his back as he walked to the car. He'd asked his parents for a Tesla, arguing his generation needed to get serious about carbon emissions since they were going to be around for another six or seven decades. His parents lauded his green side and bought him a Prius. Cars were transportation, not a status symbol, they said.

Part of him agreed. And it *was* totally awesome that they bought him a car. But sometimes his six-foot-three body needed a bit more room. Today's nearly four-hour drive was one of them. Luckily, they only had about an hour to go.

"Okay, let's—" The scowl on Luke's face as he stared at his phone made him less attractive. Nico had been down that road enough to know how it felt. It also spoke to how attached he still was to his ex. Sadly, Nico had experience with that emotion too.

Leaning on the hood of Nico's car, Luke swiped at the screen, scowling. Nico wished this Kent guy wasn't based in Philly. This summer would be buckets of fun.

Gliding to the spot next to Luke, Nico lightly smacked the back of Luke's head.

"Hey! What the fuck!"

Nico held out his hand. "Just following instructions." He wiggled his fingers for Luke to pass over the phone.

"What makes you think I'm looking at Kent's profile?"

"Seriously?" Nico arched his brow.

Luke's expression softened into defeat, and he slapped the phone into Nico's outstretched hand. "Why is it so hard to hate him?"

"Because *you* actually cared for him, even if he turned out to be a fuckwit." He logged off Luke's Facebook and offered the phone back.

"Keep it until we get to the apartment. That way for the next hour I won't be tempted to see what fun and amazing things he and his super-rich, super-hot new boyfriend are doing."

Nico stuffed the phone in one of his many pockets. "I could always ask my cousins Paulie and Nunzio to mess him up a bit."

"Your cousins are in the Mafia?"

The awe on Luke's face and in his voice almost made Nico continue the lie. "I don't even have cousins named Paulie and

Nunzio, but it sounded good. And coming from a New York Italian, people are willing to believe it's true."

"Fuck, I believed it. Sorry."

Nico laughed and hitched a thumb over his shoulder. "What do you say we get moving to make it before dark?"

CHAPTER FIVE

Nico

Nico: Holy Fuck! Parking sucks in Philly!

Elisa: Yikes! Language!

Nico: You sound more like Mama every day

Elisa: Whatever. Easy trip?

Nico: Yeah. Luke's good company. Too bad he isn't over his ex.

Nico rounded the car and met Luke at the trunk. "Here." He held out Luke's phone. "Try not to stalk Kent too much."

"Thanks." Luke shoved it into his left pocket and hurriedly snatched his laptop bag from the trunk. "We should take as much as we can carry. Don't want to leave anything in the car."

Nico smirked. "Country boy."

"What? I don't want our stuff stolen."

"Even if we carry as much as we can, we'll need to make another trip." Nico pulled his backpack with his laptop and other valuables from the back seat. "I won't leave the car here long."

"It takes seconds to break in and steal something."

"It'll be *fine*." Not that he knew what crime was like in Philadelphia. "Soon as I know where our parking space is, I'll run back like the wind and move it."

Luke cocked his head and his dark eyes washed over Nico. "Are you always this . . ." He rolled his finger. "You know."

"Dramatic?" Nico glanced over Luke's shoulder, unable to meet his eyes. So much for toning himself down. He mumbled, "That's me, I guess."

"I meant *laid back*." Luke retrieved his backpack and shut the back door. "I'm nervous as fuck moving to a big city, and you're . . . not."

Laid back. With a relieved flutter, Nico procured his own phone with directions to their apartment. "This way."

Their landlady owned and lived in the brownstone—a rowhouse in Philly parlance. Another reason New York was so much cooler. He'd take brownstone over rowhouse any day.

Mrs. Randazzo lived up to the elderly Italian grandmother stereotype. She met them in a mostly white sundress, house slippers, and granny glasses hanging from her neck on a beaded lanyard that reminded Nico of Rosary beads. Teased hair framed her dolled-up face, and her smile glittered.

"I gotta tell you boys, I feel like I won the lottery," she said in a thick South Philly accent. "I did some checking on you both. Amato's bakery, eh?"

Nico nodded. He was proud of the family business. "Yes, ma'am. My papà is the fourth generation to run the bakery."

"I love sfogliatelle. Are yours any good?"

Nico smiled at her eager interest in the pastry. "I'd stack ours up against any in the city. My sister is coming next weekend; I'll have her bring you a sampler tin."

Mrs. Randazzo half-heartedly attempted to decline, and Nico held back a knowing grin. He knew this game. Nonna had taught him well.

"I insist. It's the least I can do, given how wonderfully accommodating you've been to Luca and me."

"Aw." She grabbed his cheek and pinched, and Nico smiled through the sting. "You're a good boy."

Luke chuckled softly, drawing the landlady's and Nico's attention. He had his thumb hooked under his bag straps at his shoulder, and on his lips played a soft smile. His eyes whipped away from Nico and settled on Mrs. Randazzo, who hummed with narrowed eyes.

"And you play baseball for your school." She waved them inside, and Nico and Luke squeezed past her into a brown tiled foyer. "You ain't no Richie Ashburn, but your stats look good."

"Richie who?" Nico asked in Luke's ear, not immune to the block of heat blasting him as Luke leaned toward him.

"Fuck if I know," Luke whispered back. He cleared his throat and fixed a wide smile on Mrs. Randazzo. "I'm impressed you found that out, ma'am."

"My granddaughter might have helped." Her lips quirked. "She's disappointed you two are a couple."

Nico swung his head toward Luke, meeting equally surprised eyes. Luke frowned and palmed his nape, and Nico shifted from foot to foot. Awkward anyone? "Ah, we're not a couple. Just friends."

"Oh. *Ohhh*." She waved them into a sitting room.

The formal furniture looked like things Nico had seen in his great-aunts' and -uncles' homes. The couch was covered in thick plastic, and the pair of formal wing chairs sat across from it, separated by a glass-covered coffee table. Luke started for a chair, and Nico snagged his elbow and guided him toward the couch.

Luke shot him a look, and Nico pointedly looked at the plastic-covered sofa. "We've been driving a while. Best not to get dirt on the nice furniture." The plastic creaked under them.

Mrs. Randazzo used one of the chairs. "I thought he"—she gestured to Nico—"was the new boyfriend."

"No," Luke said quickly. Too quickly.

Nico kept the grin on his face from wobbling. "I'm overseeing the plans for my sister's wedding. Her planner cancelled on short notice. She needed a replacement, and I needed a roof over my head, and that's where Luke comes in."

"I see. Your sister lives here?"

"Not yet. Her fiancé is from here and just got an offer from a big law firm. She's moving down before the wedding."

"You know anything about planning a wedding?" she asked skeptically. Right into their business. She definitely took a page from his nonna's book. "Where are they having this?"

"The Union League." He smiled as her eyebrow shot up. "And I've planned a few events in my time. Mostly things are settled, but I'm making sure everything stays that way."

"You're a good brother." She clapped her hands together. "Well . . . the apartment only has one bedroom. Quinton and his girlfriend live together."

Nico wasn't sure where this talk of the last tenants was going, but his skin prickled. He glanced at Luke palming the plastic on either side of him.

"Right," Luke said. "He told me that when I contacted him."

"Did he tell you they recently bought a giant king-size bed that takes up most of the bedroom?" Her dark eyebrow arched.

Luke gave Nico a panicked look. "He said they had two twins that they used a bed bridge to make into a king."

Mrs. Randazzo shook her head. "They had it delivered before they left for the summer. I didn't think anything of it at the time. I assumed you two were . . . you know."

"Right," Nico said. Not the best start to the summer. "No worries. We'll figure something out."

Luke stared at his knees, strong jaw ticking. "May we see the apartment now?

Mrs. Randazzo procured a key ring. "These two work on the apartment doors—front, and back. The small ones are for the gate next to the garage. Don't leave that open. I don't want any crazies camping in the back yard."

"How do we get to the garage?" Nico asked.

"This is Pine." She pointed to the front of the house. "There's an alley that runs behind the house. The address is painted on the garage. I'll open the door before you get back. Push the button by the door into the yard to close it behind you."

"Alley behind, number on, shut when I leave. Got it." Nico gave her a broad smile. "Shouldn't be hard at all."

"Don't think so." She reclined in her chair. "Let me know when you're back, and I'll give you a remote for the garage. And if you need any suggestions on where to eat or go out, let me know."

"Thank you, Mrs. R." Luke stared at the keys, and Nico nudged him. "Do you want to go to the apartment or come with me to get the car?"

"Huh?" He blinked and stood. "I'll take your backpack with me and go to the apartment. Call me when you get here, and I'll help you unpack."

Nico nodded to their landlady. "Pleasure to meet you, Mrs. R. I know my family will be coming down at least a couple of times this summer, so you'll have to join us for dinner."

She smiled and wagged a finger at him. "You're certainly a charmer, aren't you?"

"I do what I can."

She snorted. "I'm sure you do."

Luke

Nico: At the car. No break-ins to report.

Luke: Smart ass.

LUKE HAD *NOT* AGREED to rent a bedroom with *one* bed. Why hadn't Quinton said something?

Fuck, nothing about this summer was going according to plan. He tossed his and Nico's backpacks on the king bed.

"Stupid Kent," he growled.

His phone buzzed, and his hand shot into his pocket. Oh. *Not* a new Kent status update. He should have let Nico keep his phone.

Nico: That's probably the dumbest part of my anatomy.

Some of the tension in his shoulders eased as he laughed. That creampuff was too easy to pass up.

Luke: Then get your stupid ass back here so we can unpack. :P

Nico: Here. Come get me and all our crap.

Leaving the door open, he trotted down the stairs and into the backyard. Though *backyard* was a stretch of the imagination. A brick patio took up three-quarters of the space with small flowerbeds either side. The whole apartment was smaller than the first floor of his country home.

Gonna be cozy this summer.

Nico emerged from the side door carrying what looked like half of Luke's stuff. He offered the bags to Luke. "Last in, first out. If you take these up, I'll get the next bunch."

Fifteen minutes later, they had all their bags in their bedroom.

Luke didn't dare look at Nico. "What are we going to do about this?"

"Paint a line down the center of the bed and punish any encroachment with death?"

Luke groaned and laughed. He eyed Nico and noted the slight unease in his posture. Not so laid-back now. "I'm serious."

"So was I." Nico sat on the edge of the bed and gave it a test bounce that—wow—should not have taken Luke the places it took him. "Okay, so I wasn't. But I think the solution for tonight is we both use the bed and promise to stay on our own side."

Luke shoved the unbidden images away and focused all his attention on his laptop bag. "Is there a *tomorrow* part to this solution?"

"Air mattress."

Luke sized up the room. They'd need to move the bed to create enough space, but it could work. "Who gets which?"

"Since I don't expect to be entertaining guests at night, I don't mind taking the air mattress, but I'll require a quid pro quo."

"If your price is too high, I'll resort to wrestling you for the bed."

"Oh, the things you say, Mr. DeRosa." Nico fanned his face with his right hand while actual heat rippled up Luke's throat at the unintended implication.

"Your price, Nico."

"I want the bathroom first in the morning."

"Fair deal. You take care of buying the mattress, we'll split the cost, but no dibs on the bathroom until it arrives."

"Oh, so organized." Nico's eyes danced. "Do you like to be in charge?"

Luke blinked rapidly at Nico's teasing. "Um, not really. I just like to plan ahead."

"Nothing wrong with a surprise now and then to liven things up." Nico dug out his phone. "But about the mattress. Let me get it. My parents were thinking of getting one for my brother's kids when they come for the wedding, so I can put it on the wedding bill. Now, I don't know about you, but I'm hungry. We should figure something out before it gets too late."

"I'm good. I have some ramen in my bags."

"Ramen." Nico stared blankly at him. "That won't do."

"I'm on a budget. It's why I need you splitting the cost of this . . . *cozy* apartment with me."

Nico held up a finger. "I get you're on a budget, and I won't ask you to blow it. But I like real food, *and* I like to cook. We're going food shopping, and you can kick in whatever you've budgeted, and I'll be fine."

"I can't take handouts from you." Hell, he hardly knew the guy.

"It won't be."

"So how does me letting you buy food for us both not turn into you paying for me?"

"Do you cook?"

"Huh? What's that got to do with anything?"

"*Do you cook?* And more to the point, have you ever been food shopping?"

"Not really. I mean, I can make mac and cheese from a box."

"And ramen." Nico's face wrinkled up like he'd smelled garbage on a hot summer day.

"That too." Luke chuckled.

"My point is that other than things like mac and cheese and *ramen*, it's hard to buy for one person. It's even harder to cook for one. At least the way I cook."

"Nico, I can't let you cook for me all summer."

"I won't." He swiped at his screen. "I'll cook for me—and you'll help me eat it."

"How's that different?"

"Because I won't be able to eat what I make knowing you're going eat something that came in a cup." Nico clicked off his phone and stuffed it in his pocket. "C'mon. There's a Whole Foods a few blocks away. We can discuss this while we walk."

Whole Foods? "Is there a Target or Walmart nearby?"

"Seriously?" Nico put a hand on his hip, steering Luke's gaze toward his crotch. He jerked his head back up. "You want me to buy food at Walmart or Target?"

"No, I want to buy an air mattress, and we need sheets for a king bed." Luke stared at the bare mattress in front of them. "Unless you're one of those super prepared people who brought sheets in every size."

"Oh." Nico shifted his gaze to bed. "No. I brought twin sheets like we discussed."

"So, Walmart or Target?"

"Target is closer." Nico twisted his phone so Luke could see the screen. "Not really walkable, but not too far." Nico tossed his keys, and Luke snagged them neatly from the air. "You can drive if you want."

Luke death-gripped the jagged metal. Him? Driving in the city? "Um . . . I couldn't. It's your car."

"Sure you can. I don't get crazy protective over my wheels. You're good, and I'm insured."

"It's just . . ."

Nico scrutinized Luke, careful gaze stroking his face, his posture. Luke tried to keep loose and casual, but those damn keys in his hand cut into his skin.

"On second thought," Nico said, "the electric engine takes getting used to. Might be easier if I drove."

Luke handed over the keys. Their eyes met, and Luke silently poured his thanks into the look. Nico nodded and strode out of the bedroom.

"We'll hit Target first, then get food. Then you can make the bed while I cook."

"Sounds like *you* like being in charge."

Nico glanced over his shoulder and winked, and Luke staggered with the hit of butterflies to his gut.

Oh no, no. Nope.

They were *roommates*.

Luke wouldn't mess up this summer any more than he had already.

Nico

Elisa: How's day 1 of your Philly Adventure?

Nico: About as well as things went in Priscilla, Queen of the Desert.

Elisa: LOL! I had to google that to know WTF you meant.

Nico: Here's hoping today isn't a sign of things to come.

NICO PUT the last of the pasta in a container—one of the four containers the owner had. So much for a well-stocked kitchen. Tomorrow he'd see if his mother or Nonna had a few they could part with for the summer.

He also needed to order an air mattress. Like what the fuck? How could Target *and* Walmart both be out of air mattresses?

Luke hummed as he washed the pot. If he did that every night Nico cooked, this was a match made in heaven.

"Thanks for cleaning up. It's the one part of cooking I hate."

"Shit, this is the least I can do. Dinner was amazing."

Not amazing, but okay for something made on the fly. "You're saying that because you eat at Harrison's cafeteria."

"I'm saying that because I'm about to bust." Luke patted his stomach as if dinner would do anything to change his flat abs.

"Fresher herbs would have been better." Mrs. R would know where to shop. Nico would ask in the morning.

"Better? It can *get* better?" Luke narrowed his eyes on him. "Is this your plan so I let you cook for me all summer?"

Nico laughed. "It's my master plot to avoid washing pots all summer."

"I knew dinner was too good to be true." Luke's smirk morphed into a smile and ended with a wink that had Nico's pulse skipping.

If only Luke weren't so slam-him-in-the-gut attractive. Like a sports model. Body all toned, lean muscle that bulged gently where it should, his arms. His ass . . .

Nico whipped up the threadbare piece of cloth that passed for the lone dishtowel—something else to put on the care package list—and dried the pot. When they finished cleaning, Luke snagged his arm and towed him to the table.

"Can we talk for a minute?"

Nico cringed. Those words never ended well for him. "Sure."

Luke sat and absently drew on the grainy wood with his finger. "Thanks again for dinner."

"You don't need to keep thanking me. It's no big deal."

"Yeah, well I appreciate it. And for buying the sheets."

"But?" Nico prompted.

"But you can't keep paying for me," Luke choked out.

Ah. *That.* "I didn't pay for you. I didn't want bargain sheets. I'd break out if I slept on them."

"Can we cut the jokes?" Luke shifted his gaze from the table to Nico. "I know what you're doing, and I appreciate it, but I can take care of myself."

"I know, but . . ." No but. Nico had to respect Luke's position. "I won't push it again. I'm sorry."

Luke puffed up his cheeks, blew out the air. "You're being super nice."

"But it makes you uncomfortable. Got it."

Silence stretched between them, all kinds of awkward fun.

Luke's Adam's apple jutted. "I shouldn't have taken this internship, but it was the only Big Four offer I got. And, well, there was Kent."

"What should you have done instead?"

"Taken a different offer closer to home." He shrugged. "Or gone home to work on a farm."

"Are your parents farmers?"

"God, no." Luke laughed. "We live in a subdivision. Dad's a manager for a national insurance company, and Mom's a tech at a hospital."

"Okay, so where's this farm you'd have worked on?"

"They're all around us, actually. I've always found work during the summer."

"So this year's a change for you."

"Big time." Luke's soft voice made him seem homesick.

Nico suppressed the urge to lean in and hug him. He wasn't sure where Luke stood with casual contact. Probably wouldn't welcome it, jock that he was.

Luke straightened in his chair. "My parents didn't love Kent, but they supported me taking the internship. They're helping me afford a summer with no job."

"And you don't want to keep asking them for more."

"Exactly. They already give me more than they should. Dad keeps telling me it's fine because I got a scholarship, but they need the money."

Living with Isaiah for two years, Nico totally got it.

A sad, faraway look tinted Luke's eyes. "This summer I wanted to prove I can be independent."

Curiosity gnawed at Nico. "Why?"

Luke paused as if weighing how much to share. Vulnerability glinted in his eyes, and Nico wished he'd kept his mouth shut. "You don't have to answer that—"

"My sister is autistic, and it's unlikely she'll be able to live on her own. Their biggest fear is what will happen when they're gone."

Nico held back a flood of questions. His picture of Luke became fuller with every hour they spent together—and Nico liked the glimpses of the man he saw inside. "Okay. I can see that."

"My parents have been balancing saving for her future and helping me. They feel that they should give us equal." He shook his head vehemently. "I don't need equal. Rosalie needs to be their focus."

"And you wanted them to see they *could* focus on your sister."

"Yet every decision I've made does the opposite."

"Luke . . ." Nico floundered for the right words. "I'll be more sensitive to your situation."

"You're fine. Really." Luke perked up and flashed him a grin. "Your excuses suck, though. No one breaks out in hives from cheap sheets."

"No, but do *you* need king-size sheets?"

"Ah, no."

"Me neither. I figure I'll send them home when we go back to school, but Nonna would never use ones with low thread count."

"Low what?"

"Thread count. The higher the count, the better the quality of the fabric."

Luke looked skeptical. "I never knew that."

"It's true. So it would've been a waste of money if we'd bought something Nonna would never use." That, and she'd give Nico the business for not spending wisely. Quality before quantity, always.

Luke eyed Nico quietly. "Can I ask you something?"

"Why am I afraid?"

Luke laughed, low and creamy. "Because you're a paranoid city boy?"

Nico crossed his arms. "That's so me. What's your question, country boy?"

"You talk way more about your grandparents than your parents. What's up with that?"

"Ah, that." Nico kept his tone light. "Got a minute?"

"Want me to make coffee?"

"Are you any good at it? You think *ramen* is a meal."

"Funny. I can handle coffee." He popped up and opened the cabinet where they'd stashed the coffee. "Talk while I measure."

"I think you like being in charge, too." Luke reddened, and Nico smiled innocently. "The bakery has been in the family for four generations. Five if you count me. But things are very different now than they were even thirty-five years ago when Nonno's father died. My grandfather didn't adapt to change very well.

"Nonno is an amazing pastry chef and baker, but a lousy business owner. He'd make too much of one thing that didn't sell and not enough of what people wanted. He'd order too much butter and it'd go bad, but they never had enough flour or sugar. People wanted premium coffee and he stuck with the cheaper stuff. That kind of thing. And he was terrible at managing employees."

"Wow, dude. Don't hold back." Luke glanced up from scooping grounds into the basket. "I thought you liked him?"

"I love him to death. Who do you think told me all this?"

"Really?"

"Yep. He knew he was killing the business, but like all Amatos, he wouldn't ask for help. Finally, Nonna stepped in."

"Wasn't she helping him run the business?"

"Oh, heavens no. Nonno was *old school* Italian. His wife did not work. She ruled the house. When I was five, she called a family meeting with my father and his two sisters. She explained the situation and asked her children if they wanted to keep the business or sell it. My aunts don't work and had no interest in helping run the business, so they voted to sell. My father was already working there, trying to fix things, but so long as Nonno was in charge, he could only do so much. He voted to keep it."

"So your dad bought out his sisters." Luke opened two cabinet doors before taking down two mugs.

"No and yes." Nico moved into the kitchen to wait for the coffee to finish. "Nonna and Nonno had bought out Nonno's siblings years ago— they owned the business. They appointed my dad to run it and began transferring ownership to him as part of his salary."

"Bet that went over well."

"Like a drag brunch without alcohol." Nico snapped his right hand, and immediately scolded himself. He was supposed to tone that down.

Luke eyed him, his hand, his stupid cargo shorts and shirt, and frowned. "Like what?"

"It didn't go over well."

"Did you say like a drag brunch?"

Nico tapped the coffeepot as if that would make it finish sooner. "That was a bit much, I suppose."

"There's such a thing?"

"Huh?"

"Drag brunch. That exists?"

Where had this guy been? "Yeah. I went to a few in New York. To eat."

"Do they have those in Philly?"

Not the conversation he expected to have on their first night in the apartment. "Maybe. I never checked."

"We should go if they have one." He reached for the coffeepot, then stopped. "If it's not too expensive."

"Okay, sure." Unexpected, but—

"Awesome."

Yeah, awesome.

Luke removed the pot and filled both cups. "You were telling me about your parents."

"Right." Nico sipped and stared at Luke over the lip of the cup. "Once Papà took over, he realized two things. One, the business was worse than he expected. And two, he couldn't manage the bakery and the financial side alone. Which meant he needed help. Since my aunts weren't interested, he got my mom to help him."

"I take it your mom didn't work before that?"

"She did before my older brother was born."

"Your grandfather was okay with that?"

"That was one of Papà's conditions for taking over. He also said Nonno had to remain in the business as head pastry chef and Nonna had to help watch me and my siblings."

Luke gulped his coffee. "You spent more time with your gran—nonna—growing up."

"Yep. And being the baby of the family, I'm her favorite."

"Must be your incredible modesty."

"Whatever." Nico hid a smirk in another sip. "Okay, you did a good job with this."

Luke picked up the bag. "I think it's the coffee we bought. I never heard of Lavazza, but I like it."

"Well the bag does say it's Italy's favorite." Nico shrugged. "It's pretty good."

A smile stretched Luke's lips. "You totally bought it because it said that, didn't you?"

Nico tried to play it straight but couldn't hold back the goofy grin. "Busted. But hey, it turned out to be good, right?"

Luke nodded once and raised his cup. "Here's to the rest of the summer turning out good, too."

Nico inched his mug higher. "And to our first night!"

NICO PUT his toothbrush in the holder and clicked off the light. The one in the bedroom glowed into the hall, easing the way, but not easing his nerves. He hadn't shared a bed with a guy that he wasn't sleeping with since he was six. And Joey Virgosia's family was so close to his, they were like relatives.

Pulling back the sheet, he kept his eyes on his side of the bed. Not that it mattered. Luke had gotten in before him and lay on his side facing the wall. He couldn't nail down what weirded him out most. That he barely knew Luke, or that he was sharing a bed with a totally hot, single gay guy and they wouldn't do anything but sleep.

He turned off the lamp on the nightstand, rolled onto his back, and stared at the darkened ceiling.

Don't think about how hot he is. Don't think about how sweet he might possibly be.

Oh God, Luke—*jock* Luke—was afraid to drive in the big city. He wanted to prove himself to show his parents he'd be there for his sister.

Nico was big in trouble.

He turned on his side, back to Luke.

So what if Nico liked the guy? That didn't mean anything would happen. Dating someone who still had a thing for their ex was like flicking a lighter around flammable liquid. It never ended well.

Plus, he'd seen Luke frown when he got campy. Luke would never seriously go for someone like Nico.

They could be friends—maybe even good friends—but that was it.

Absolutely it.

CHAPTER SIX

Luke

Kent: What's the room # we're meeting at tomorrow?

Luke: Seriously?

Kent: Yeah, I can't find the email.

Luke: 27th floor, room 42. 9 am.

Kent: Thanks! Knew you'd know it. You're always so organized.

That was him, always with the information handy.

Luke set the phone on the table and closed his laptop. No wonder Kent thought he was boring.

He should have ignored Kent's message. Or at least made him sweat an hour.

He stretched his neck, sore from sleeping so stiffly.

"Seriously, E? It's *Sunday*!" Nico's voice carried into the kitchen from the bedroom. "Fine. Send it, and I'll look at it. *Later.* Luke and I are going shopping today."

Luke gulped the fresh batch of coffee he'd brewed. Nico had suggested they go to the Italian market, but should he? His stomach was a knotted mess. Tomorrow, the rest of his life began.

Only 10 percent of interns got offers, according to the career development office at Harrison, and Luke was determined to be one of them.

"Why would I have talked to the asshole? *He* dumped *me.*" Nico's voice grew distant. The bathroom door snicked shut, muffling the rest of his words.

The easy way Nico bantered with his sister had Luke yearning for the same, for home. Maybe he could squeeze in a trip home before school started? Finances permitting.

"Okay. I'll call tonight if I have any questions," Nico said as he emerged into the kitchen a few moments later. His fiery, bemused gaze hit Luke's with warmth and frustration. "Ugh. My sister is crazy."

"I heard." Luke suppressed a smile. "What's wrong?"

Nico tugged the rim of his light blue polo shirt that sat upon brown khakis. The sleeves stretched around his biceps, showing off considerable definition. But that wasn't what sparked Luke's curiosity.

This made two days in a row Nico had worn obviously newly bought clothes. New, yet plainer than he'd first seen on the guy. Something about it didn't sit right with Luke—maybe the way the clothes didn't sit right on Nico.

Not that he looked bad—that would make summer easier—no, the clothes looked comfortable. Just that Nico looked uncomfortable in them.

Nico stopped fiddling with his shirt and poured coffee into a mug. "Wrong? Nothing and everything. She's at home. Elliott's here in Philly studying for the bar exam, and she has nothing else to do except nitpick about wedding details."

The chair skidded as Luke got up with his empty cup. "It *is* her wedding, and she *did* hire you to be the planner."

Nico snorted. "If I were a real wedding planner, there's no way she'd call me on a Sunday. She's taking full advantage of the fact I love her to death."

Luke raised an eyebrow. "Could've fooled me."

"Pfft. That's just how we talk." Nico took a long sip and eyed Luke. "I poked my head in and you were scowling at your phone. Everything alright?"

Luke grimaced. "Fine. Kent lost the orientation email with tomorrow's details."

"I hope you gave him the wrong room and told him to report two hours late."

He should have, but that wasn't him. "Nope?"

Nico gaped at him. "You *gave him the details*?"

"Seemed the right thing to do." At the time. Now he wished he hadn't jumped to help Kent like that. Luke stared hard at the coffee swishing in his mug.

Nico leaned against the counter next to him and bumped Luke's shoulder. "Hey, you were the bigger person. Something I might need to work on."

Luke peeked at him out the corner of his eye. "Oh?"

"I *might* have written 'fucker' on my ex's pillow before I left campus."

"Might?" Luke lifted his mug, his arm brushing Nico's again. "You don't know?"

Nico downed the last of his coffee and lurched toward the sink. "I think I've said enough."

A laugh shot from deep inside. "You can't refuse to answer. A roommate needs to know."

"I have a constitutional right to remain silent and I'm exercising that right. And"—he pointed to Luke—"you're not allowed to draw any adverse inference from my silence."

Luke stared at Nico in disbelief and snorted. "Professor Meadows, constitutional law?"

"Last semester. You?"

"Last spring." Luke rolled his eyes. "Man, he was so . . ."

"Boring?"

"Yeah." *Just like me.* He dropped his mug into the sink next to Nico's and washed them both. "So I hear we're shopping?"

Nico whistled playfully, avoiding eye contact.

Luke chuckled, and Nico folded, sagging against the counter beside him. "It's easier to get off the phone when someone's waiting on you."

"True." Luke dried their mugs and opened the cupboard above Nico. Startled breath fizzled over his neck, and Luke froze at their proximity. Their eyes clashed, and Luke tried not to read into the way Nico looked at him, that cautious spark in his eye. Heat from Nico blazed into him, frying his nerve endings, and Luke dropped the mugs onto the shelf and jerked back. "So. Where are we going?"

Nico raced a hand through his hair. "We?"

"Well, I don't want to make a liar out of you." Also, sitting in the apartment and stewing didn't exactly light him with enthusiasm. "You've already taken the Fifth once today."

"Keep this up, and you'll end up my consigliere." Nico stuck his head into the closet and came out with a pair of reusable bags. "I need to talk to Quinton about false advertising. This is *not* a fully stocked kitchen."

"Maybe not for you, but it works for us common folk. You're just beyond the rest of us, Nico."

"Guess I am a bit much." A flash of emotion crossed Nico's face, and he twisted away from Luke. "To answer your question, there's a farmers' market in South Philly I want to check out. That's Philly's Little Italy."

"Oh." Maybe stewing in his own shortcomings didn't sound so bad after all.

Nico read his hesitance and tugged his arm. “C’mon, it won’t be so bad. These things have way more than just produce.”

“Yeah?”

“Totally. And if you’re still disappointed, we can stop by one of the bakeries and I can impress you with my knowledge of Italian pastries.”

That sounded way more appealing to Luke. “Deal.”

Nico

Nico: Ugh! The farmers’ markets here are glorified grocery stores. Are you sure you want to move here?

Elisa: I’m not moving for the food.

Nico: I get that, but love only gets you so far.

Elisa: lol! Whatever you say, boo.

“Grr!” He shoved his phone in his pocket.

“What’s wrong?” Luke asked.

“My know-it-all sister.” She wasn’t really, but talking about being in love was salt in his very fresh wound.

“Did you tell her she should reconsider marriage because the markets are pathetic?”

“I didn’t use the word *pathetic*.” He feigned interest in an eggplant. “I’m only half kidding. Like so much here, the markets are different. There’s good stuff here, but the atmosphere is more commercial than I’m used to back home.”

“You don’t want to know what I consider a farmers’ market.” Luke raised his eyebrow in challenge.

“On my God! Right.” Nico moved to the next vendor. “So tell

me, big country, do they milk the cows and churn the butter on the grounds at your markets?"

"Funny guy." Luke narrowed his eyes on him, failing to hide his grin. "Like you said, it's different. Where I live, most of the vendors are the farmers. And it's outside under a tent."

"Did you have to work at them?" The image of Luke in overalls with a bit of straw in his mouth had his brain working overtime, and the shivers from their *moment* earlier flooded back to him.

"Of course. The hired hands help give the family a break."

"My synapses are going crazy."

"Huh?"

"You and all those hot farm boys working under a tent. Did you, you know, ever hook up with one of them?"

Luke reddened.

"Okay, so that's a yes." Nico's smile threatened to split his face, and something else threatened to split his shorts. "You totally need to dish."

"Are you gonna share your bakery hookups?"

Adorable how he tried to deflect it back onto Nico. But not going to work. "Had I any, I would, but I lived in New York City. I didn't need to hook up with someone who worked for the family."

"Like there wasn't anyone who worked there that got you fired up."

"Different question. And you're evading. Indulge me with your farm-boy love story."

Luke's rosy cheeks deepened to the color of turnips, and how he squirmed. God, Nico so badly wanted to know . . .

"Never mind," Nico coughed out. "It's none of my business. How about we get coffee and a pastry. My treat for being such a tool."

"You're not a tool." Luke visibly relaxed. "Coffee sounds good, but you don't need to pay."

"It's no big deal." Luke's jaw tightened, and Nico chastised himself for the thoughtless offer. "I mean, no treat, but can I at least demonstrate my pastry expertise?"

"Since I can't pronounce half of what I saw, that would be great."

"Deal." He pointed back the way they'd come. "That bakery on the corner looked promising."

"It rates the Amato stamp of approval?"

"I said *promising*." Nico winked. "Taste will determine if it gets a thumbs-up."

"Of course." Luke cheerily thumped Nico on the back, hand lingering long enough that Nico would feel the imprint the rest of the day. "I'll let you take point."

The Esposito's bakery stall looked authentic enough. Three older ladies in white coats used metal cookie sheets to collect orders. Just like the storefront back home.

"What can I get you, hon?" Estelle—according to her name tag—peered at him over tortoise-rimmed glasses.

"Can I get four sfogliatelle, six cannoli, and some pignoli, please?"

She raised an eyebrow. "Sure, hon. Do you want those cannoli filled or to take home?"

"Filled, please. We'll eat them before they get soggy."

"Why are you getting so much?" Luke asked.

"Two sfogliatelle and two cannolis are for Mrs. R. She seems to like her sweets."

"Charmer," Luke said, sounding too much like Mrs. Randazzo for it to be coincidence.

"She knows everything that happens in the neighborhood. I want to be on her good side."

Luke laughed. "Nah, you're just a nice guy who wants to make her day."

Nico shrugged, ticklish at the thought Luke read him like

that, and pulled his gaze back to Estelle. "How do you sell your pignoli?"

"However you want, hon. We can do a tin if you like, or by the pound."

"No tin." His sister would bring plenty next weekend. "How about six?"

"Sure thing." She looked at him again. "Brooklyn?"

Nico beamed and glimpsed Luke smiling beside him. "How'd you know?"

"The way you say sfogliatelle and pignoli." He noted the slight difference in her accent. "My grandmother was from Brooklyn, and that's how she said them."

"Nico's family owns a bakery in Brooklyn," Luke said.

"Oh?" Estelle looked from Nico to Luke and back. "Which one?"

Nico shot Luke a look. "Amato's."

"Really?" She said it like she knew the name. "Checking out the competition?"

"No. Just getting some pastries. My friend hasn't tried sfogliatelle before."

"You came to the right place." She grabbed a tray and some tongs. "We make the best in Philadelphia."

Nico winked at Luke. "I can't wait to try them. Can you give us two paper plates so we can eat some here?"

She nodded and boxed up their order. "You let me know what you think."

"Of course." He could see her telling people how one of the Amatos from New York raved about their pastry.

"Is that all?"

"Two small coffees?" Luke said, holding out his credit card.

"I got this," Nico said, handing his card to Estelle. She looked at them, and Nico waved his card a bit closer. When she took his card, Nico ignored the daggers Luke shot. When he heard what this would cost, he'd be glad he let Nico pay.

"I was going to get it," Luke said, miffed.

"We can settle later." Nico pointed to the overhead menu with the prices. "These aren't donuts or croissants at a coffee shop."

"The total is forty-three seventy-five." Estelle handed Nico back his card. "I tossed in the coffees for free."

Nico cocked his head. "Mrs. Esposito?"

"What gave it away?" She chuckled.

"Nonno would fire anyone who gave something away. That's his job." He held out his hand. "Nicodemo Amato. Pleased to meet you."

"Same." She handed him the bag. "Enjoy, and come back and see us again."

"Oh, I'm sure we'll be back." Nico snagged a plastic knife and some napkins while Luke grabbed their coffee.

The market had a seating area that was mostly full. They found a small table close to the bakery and sat in the wrought iron chairs. Before Luke could speak, Nico held up a finger.

"I'm sorry for paying, but I was afraid you didn't know how expensive this was going to be." He worried the top of his coffee cup and finally glanced up. "You pay for coffee another time?"

Luke rubbed his nape. A tic, Nico decided. Something he did when he wasn't sure what to say or how to say it. It was cute on the jock.

"You're right," Luke said. "I had no idea. Is that what you guys charge?"

"Yeah, at the bakery. It's more if you order online." He took one sfogliatelle and one of the cannoli from their boxes and put them on one plate.

"You gonna eat both of them?"

"Not a chance." Nico held up the knife before he started to cut. "I figured we'd start with half of each. Once you see how filling they are, you may not want any more."

He used the knife to push half of each pastry onto a plate. He tried to slide one half with the knife but it started to topple, and

Nico instinctively balanced it with his fingers. "Sorry about the fingers."

"I'm not a germaphobe."

Nico picked up his half of the sfogliatelle, watching Luke carefully do the same. "Let's see how it tastes."

Luke smiled. "Ah, the Amato stamp of approval."

The first bite crunched like it should, and his mouth filled with flaky crust and sweet cheese. He hummed his approval and glanced at Luke, who was already going for his second bite, a blissed-out look on his face. "Wow. This is—"

"Luke?"

They turned toward the voice, and Nico recognized the two guys from Luke's Facebook page immediately. Luke's ex, and Luke's ex's new boyfriend.

Luke

WHEN LUKE REALIZED Kent and his new boyfriend stood less than six feet from him and Nico, his good spirits dropped out of his feet and left him frozen. Kent was here, at the market. Kent and his rugged handsome face with that cocky smile Luke used to find endearing.

Kent's smile deepened—slimy, that's what it was—and he glanced at the boy hugging his arm.

Sebastian was—wow, he was really good-looking in person. There went the hope that he filtered his photos. He was a touch shorter than Luke expected, but otherwise just like the pictures in Kent's Facebook posts. Perfectly styled brown hair, tan, and well dressed. Not as well as Nico had been when Luke first saw him, but neat.

Luke continued to stare, and Nico shifted in his peripheral

vision. A foot tapped his under the table, lurching Luke into action.

"Kent." Luke glanced at Nico, who threw daggers at Kent on his behalf, foot still casually pressed up against Luke's. "What are you doing here?"

"I was going to ask you the same thing." Kent gazed at his new boyfriend, hearts in his eyes. "Sebastian was showing me one of his favorite bakeries."

Kent turned his attention back to Luke and then swiveled to Nico, his brow quirking.

Luke jumped. "Oh, right. Kent, this is Nico. Nico, Kent."

Nico's foot moved, stirring air around Luke's ankle, and Luke weirdly missed the slight pressure.

Nico stood and held out his hand. "Nice to meet you."

Right. Standing. Maybe Luke should too.

He pushed to his feet, awkwardness settling heavily on his chest, his shoulders.

Kent's eyes swept over Nico, and Luke noted the subtle change in his demeanor. "Same."

Kent introduced Sebastian, and the entire stiff exchange made Luke uneasy.

Luke hadn't meant to imply there was anything between him and Nico, but the way Kent watched them, that's what he thought.

Nico tensed at Kent's dirty look, then met Luke's gaze. He smiled broadly, moving closer until his hand brushed Luke's. Tiny sparks skittered along his skin, and it fueled Luke enough to keep his head high.

"How long have you two been dating?" Nico asked Sebastian.

"About three months."

Three *months*? Luke cut a look to Kent, who avoided his eyes, cheeks blazing.

"That's great," Nico said tightly. Like he'd done the math, too. "Congrats."

"How about you two?" Kent asked rigidly.

Nico grazed his knuckles over the back of Luke's hand, then hooked their index fingers together. "Oh, not as long as you," Nico said, squeezing Luke gently as if to say *sorry*, or *play along*. Or both. "We're in the fun stage."

Luke's voice came out an octave higher than normal. "We're getting to know each other. Well."

"Really, really well," Nico added with a sly, sexy smile Luke's way. Luke felt the effects ripple through him. *Damn, Nico*. Potent.

"Well, we should get going." Kent tugged Sebastian toward Esposito's.

"Nice meeting you two." Nico's friendly wave seemed to irk Kent into retreating faster.

"See you tomorrow," Luke muttered. He waited until they were out of earshot and exhaled. "Talk about awkward."

"Just a bit. Sorry about the three-month revelation."

Luke sighed and slumped back into his seat. "Yeah, well. I guess I'm not surprised." He still felt the ghost of Nico's touch on his foot, the back of his hand, and tight at the base of his index finger. "Thanks for . . . you know."

Nico nodded, a gentle blush on his cheeks, and returned to his sfogliatelle. "Kent clearly did not like that you'd moved on."

"You caught that too?"

Nico chewed for a minute. "He may as well have it written in permanent marker over his forehead."

"You and permanent marker," Luke said, shaking his head, a grin pulling at his lips. From the corner of his eye, he caught Kent kissing Sebastian and groaned, stomach roiling. "Fuck, why do I care so much?" He looked desperately at Nico. "How did you get over your breakup so fast?"

Nico looked at his pastry and set it down. His face tightened as he played with the lid of his coffee. "I haven't. I just hide it better."

Not what Luke expected.

Exhaling loudly, Nico looked at him, sadness swirling in his brown eyes. He shrugged. "I've broken up with guys before, but this one really hurt. I'm still processing it. Part of the reason I agreed to come to Philadelphia was to work through what happened."

Something itched in Luke to take Nico in his arms and hold him. Protect him from anyone who could lessen his spark, even for a moment. He settled on nudging his foot against Nico's. "That's his loss."

Nico gave him a half smile. "Life happens, right?

"Yeah." They ate more of the sfogliatelle. A splotch of cream stuck to Nico's lip, and Luke reached over and gently rubbed it off, freezing when he noticed what he was doing. Nico watched him cautiously, big brown eyes that had experienced far more in the dating world than Luke had, and Luke jerked his hand back, willing the heat at his throat to subside. "Ah, thanks for pretending. I owe you."

The wariness leaked out of Nico, and he shrugged, grinning. "Someday, and that day may be soon, I will call upon you to do favor for me. But until that day, accept this gesture as a gift in honor of my sister's wedding."

Nico sounded just like Marlon Brando in *The Godfather*. "You're sure you're not part of a family?"

"No," Nico continued the imitation. "But I'm serious about you owing me."

Luke played along, staring hard into Nico's eyes. He pushed Nico's plate back. "Fine, Godfather. What's your verdict on the sfogliatelle?"

CHAPTER SEVEN

Nico

Elisa: Change of plans next weekend. You need to come home. Nonna wants to have a family dinner.

Nico: Why?

Elisa: She didn't say, but I think she wants to meet your boyfriend before the wedding.

Nico: So would I.

Nico tossed his phone onto the cushion next to him. Why did everything have to be a struggle? The reason he came to Philadelphia was to avoid talking about his nonexistent love life with his family. Everyone else took the hint, but not his grandmother. He loved Nonna, but she didn't know when to stop.

He reviewed the materials from the florist. The flowers the planner had picked for the tables didn't go with the type of reception his sister wanted. Elisa would have the final say, but he wanted to give her some different options.

The bakery wasn't his favorite either. They felt too commercial, less family focused. Esposito's website said they made wedding cakes, and he put a visit to their shop on tomorrow's list of things to do.

Checking the time—five thirty—he wondered when Luke would be home. *If* he'd be home. Maybe his summer intern class would go out together, or the firm would take them to dinner. Either way, Nico didn't feel right texting to ask. They were just roommates.

Roommates. He needed to remind himself of that.

Sure, there had been some startling electricity between them, but he wasn't ready to jump into something new. Wasn't ready to get burned by another jock so soon.

Besides, Luke still had it bad for his ex. Nico wouldn't piss on Tomas if he was on fire. Luke would bring the fire department to help Kent.

He'd bet good money Sebastian would figure Kent out sooner rather than later. Three guesses where Kent would come running when that happened.

Way too messy.

He uncoiled himself from the couch, dragged his stiff limbs to the bedroom, and changed into his running clothes.

He tucked his right leg under him and began to stretch. A run would do him a world of good.

A BIT AFTER SIX THIRTY, Nico let his thoroughly sweaty self into the apartment. He'd have been home fifteen minutes sooner if Mrs. R hadn't stopped to thank him for the pastries. Fifteen minutes to say what he could have said in fifteen seconds. But she was alone, so he listened with a smile. Not like he had big plans for Monday night.

He'd just gotten under the shower spray when Luke announced his return.

"I'm home."

"How was your first day?" He almost added "dear" at the end but wasn't sure Luke would get his humor.

"Good, bad, great, interesting, take your pick." From the sound of his voice, Luke had entered the bathroom. "Hey, would it gross you out if I peed while you're in there? I really need to go."

"No, as long as I don't see it." He wouldn't mind seeing *it,* just not while Luke was peeing.

"Really? And here I got the impression you were into that kind of kink."

Before Nico could poke his head out of the curtain, he heard the telltale sound that kept him behind the opaque vinyl sheet. "I don't know where you get your information, Mr. DeRosa, but it is sorely lacking."

His southern belle voice laced with a New York accent earned him the desired laugh.

"Yes, Ms. Scarlett." The toilet flushed, and Nico thought he heard Luke leave. The voice from the bedroom confirmed it. "Did you go for a run?"

"Oh, shit," he whispered. He'd left his sweaty clothes all over the floor. "Sorry, I didn't expect you back."

"I figured." Luke sounded closer. "How was it?"

"It's a work in progress." He rinsed the last of the soap from his body. "I need to find a route with fewer lights. And a better time to go. Too many people on the sidewalk."

"Yeah, I can imagine."

Nico shut off the water and pulled back the curtain. The door closed as he reached for his towel.

After drying off and combing his hair, Nico wrapped the towel around his waist. When he exited the bathroom, Luke was in the bedroom pulling on a T-shirt.

"Sorry again." Nico scooped up his sweaty clothes and stuffed them into a laundry bag.

"No worries, really." Luke carefully put his suit pants through the hanger, his back to Nico. "How'd day one of being a wedding planner go?"

"Pretty good. I don't like the bakery the last planner chose, and I'm pretty sure my sister won't like the flowers."

"That's a good day?" Luke hung his suit in the closet. "Sounds like the old planner did a crap job."

"More a matter of taste." He shucked the towel and stepped into clean boxer briefs. "I know Elisa better. The venue is top-notch, and the band will be fine. They know all the Italian favorites and promise to play the Tarantella. Not that my family has any idea how to actually do the folk dance. They just hold hands and dance around in a circle."

"That's more than I'd know to do. I've never heard of it." Luke turned around and paused, bottom lip dropping. After a few seconds, he blinked. "I guess it wasn't such a bad day."

Nico thought Luke started to blush, but it could've been the lighting in the bedroom. "Nope, not bad, but I'm worried I won't have much to do most of the summer. There isn't *that* much work to do."

Luke's gaze skittered over Nico's length like a feather. Nico shivered, and Luke quickly pinned his eyes to a point over Nico's shoulder. "So what'll you do? Go home?"

In a world only Nico lived in, he heard disappointment in Luke's voice at the thought of Nico leaving. He pulled a black T-shirt over his head. "No way. Maybe I'll get a part-time job. I'm sure someone will vouch for my bakery bona fides."

"You'd work for the enemy?"

"Pfft. Enemy Shemeny. Philadelphia and New York are different worlds. But I doubt anyone would hire me for ten weeks." Searching through his bags, he found some shorts. "Oh, I ordered the air mattress today. Should be here by the end of the week."

"End of the week?" Clearly not what Luke expected.

Nico winced, playing with the cords of his shorts. "I couldn't find any sellers on Amazon Prime for the one I wanted. And from the three sellers that had it in stock, anything other than standard shipping was thirty dollars and up. I couldn't justify paying that for a seventy-five-dollar mattress."

"Wow, that is a lot." Luke eyed the bed. "No biggie. I haven't noticed any encroaching violations so far."

"Yeah, me neither." The bed was so big, he'd have trouble touching Luke even if he tried.

"Seriously, that's fine. I mean, I appreciate not having to kick in anything. I sure as hell don't have fifty dollars to throw away."

Nico breathed out a silent sigh. "Cool."

"I'm going to go check my email."

"Gotcha. Be out in a second."

Luke

Kent: Why didn't you meet me for lunch?

Luke: In case you missed it, we're not dating anymore.

Kent: So we're not friends either?

Luke: IDK. Are you going to explain how you've been dating Seb for three months?

"FUCKER." Luke squeezed the phone to stop himself from throwing it against the wall.

It shouldn't surprise him. That was Kent's way. Deflect and ignore. He'd done it enough when they were dating, but Luke hadn't really thought it through. Until now.

"Something wrong?" Nico padded barefoot into the kitchen.

"The usual." He shrugged. "Kent."

"Ah." He seemed to want to say more but didn't.

Probably wanted to remind Luke he'd suggested blocking Kent. Why hadn't he barred Kent from calling? Now more than ever, it was a one-sided relationship. Nico was right. He should've given the jerk the wrong intern info.

"So can you explain why your day was 'good, bad, great, and interesting?'" Nico crossed his arms and leaned against the thin wall that separated the kitchen from the rest of the apartment.

"Hmm, let's see." Luke stood and dropped the phone on the couch in case Kent responded. He didn't care what answer he gave, it would probably be a lie. "Good equals getting there on time, checking in without a problem, and finding my mentor before the orientation started."

"Definitely good." Nico pushed off the wall and took the three steps back into the kitchen. "I'm making lemon chicken, rice, and broccoli if you'd like to eat with me."

"Sounds so much better than a cup of noodles. How can I help? I'm not a total loss in the cooking department if I know what to do."

"No?"

"Nope."

"Hmm. And I was so sure you preferred giving orders to taking them." Meeting Luke's gaze, eyes twinkling with humor, Nico slid over the broccoli and cutting board. "Can you cut that into florets?"

Luke smiled. "I'm a pro at cutting and chopping."

"Perfect. And if you promise not to cut yourself, I can show you how simple it is to make the chicken."

"Scout's honor." He held up the first three fingers of his right hand. "Heck, if I come home and can make chicken, my mom won't know who I am."

"We all grow up at some point." Nico put a small pan on the stove. "Four tablespoons of butter and three tablespoons of soy sauce. Set the burner on the lowest setting."

Luke stopped cutting to take mental notes.

"Put the chicken breasts in a baking dish and season with lemon pepper." He sprinkled the meat until both sides were covered.

"You had them do something to the chicken when we ordered it. What was that?"

Nico held up one finger. "Right. Thin-sliced breast cooks faster and more evenly."

"I'm still amazed you can do all this." Luke went back to chopping while Nico swirled the contents of the pan. "I mean, my mom's a good cook, but to hear Dad talk, the early years were not so edible."

"Your mom cooked and all you can manage is stuff from a box?"

"I, ah, didn't have a lot of time to watch her." He kept his eyes on the broccoli, avoiding Nico's eyes. "If I wasn't at school, I helped take care of my sister."

"Oh wow, sorry for being so snarky. How are things now that you're away at school?"

"They're managing okay." Luke finally looked at Nico. "Rosalie is old enough now that she doesn't need as much attention as before."

"Gotcha." He opened a cabinet, pulled out a round bottle, and showed it to Luke. "The most important part to great lemon chicken."

Luke snorted. "What's that? Some super-secret Amato sauce or something?"

"Hardly. It's called Lemon Goddess dressing. The chicken tastes so much better than if you just use the lemon pepper." Nico shook the bottle quickly and then poured some over the chicken. "I believe you were explaining your day and stopped at good."

"Right." He put the chopped vegetables in a bowl and watched Nico cover the chicken in the butter-soy sauce. "Bad because Kent wanted to talk during the break. Great because the partner I'll be working with pulled me aside before Kent could talk to me. And interesting because I'm one of only a few interns that was assigned a partner."

"Really? Did everyone else have to share a mentor?"

"No, most people were assigned senior associates." One of them being Kent.

"And what is Mr. Partner like?"

"From my one whole day of working for him, Mr. Rayner seems super nice. He's shown me a few things already for projects he wants me to work on."

"That's awesome." Nico held out his fist and sounded more excited than Luke. "Sounds like they know who the superstars are already."

"I don't know about that, but I've heard more than a few people are jealous." Including Kent. "I also don't think I should read too much into it. From my conversations with Mr. Rayner, he's been mentoring interns since he was an associate and enjoys it. I think it was just random placement that landed me with him."

"Still, having the ears and eyes of a partner can't hurt your chances." Nico continued to smile.

"Probably true." So long as he didn't screw up.

LUKE PUSHED BACK from the table, almost too full to move. "That was amazing."

"Better than mac and cheese from a box?" Nico's phone buzzed on the table near him. He leaned over and read the screen.

"Way better. I feel like I'm at home."

"Right." Nico stood and grabbed their plates. "Home."

Luke almost grabbed Nico's phone to look at the message as his friend walked to the sink. Whatever he'd read flattened his mood.

"Everything okay?"

"Huh?" Nico turned on the water and glanced over.

"I asked if you're okay. You read something on your phone and now you look . . . different."

"That? No, everything's fine." He rinsed off the plates and put them in the dishwasher. "My sister isn't coming down this weekend. Her fiancé is going to New York."

Luke carried the serving dishes into the kitchen. "Oh, no. Mrs. R isn't going to get the world-famous Amato Pastry Sampler you promised her."

"No, she'll get them. I'm supposed to go up too." Nico continued to clean in silence.

"Okay, now I know something is wrong."

Nico stopped and looked over. "What?"

"You're washing the pots." He pointed at the soapy baking dish in Nico's hands. "You said the plan was you cook, I clean."

"I was only kidding about that. Besides, you helped cook."

"What's going on?" What was it Nico had said? Amato men never asked for help. "Can I help?"

Nico sighed. "Um . . . maybe."

Luke leaned against the counter so Nico couldn't avoid him.

"Nothing's wrong, it's just . . ." Nico stared hard at Luke, a tiny frown creasing his brow. Something flashed in his eyes, and his cheeks colored. Nico fidgeted with the sponge and hummed. "Remember when I said I might call in the favor from yesterday?"

Luke's stomach lurched. "Uh-huh."

"Well, I . . . the thing is." Nico put the sponge down and wiped his hands on the towel. "First, if you can't, it's not a problem. I don't want you to feel obligated or anything."

"Nico." Luke grabbed him by the shoulders. He'd never seen Nico so flustered. "Just spit it out."

"Nonna wants me to come home for a family dinner."

Luke rolled his hand in between them. "And?"

"They want me to bring my boyfriend."

Nico

Nonna: Will you and your boyfriend be coming Friday evening or Saturday morning?

Of course Nonna assumed he'd come up. It was never a question. The boyfriend thing slapped him in the face, though. He never should have told Nonna he was dating anyone.

He never should have thought it would work out with Tomas.

"Your boyfriend?" Luke leaned against the counter with casual, easy grace, crossing his arms. "But you don't have a boyfriend."

"She thinks you're the guy I was dating last semester." Nico flashed him an embarrassed grin. "I never told her his name."

Luke cocked his head, piecing the unspoken question together, probably.

Nico flushed. "Nonna wants to have a family dinner now that Elliott and I are finished with school."

Which wasn't totally accurate. This was a thinly veiled way to meet Nico's boyfriend.

Confusion colored Luke's voice. "Your family thinks we're dating?"

"Not all of them. Elisa knows you're just a friend I'm staying with. I never told my parents or grandparents Tomas and I broke up. I guess they assume that because I'm staying with someone from Harrison, he's my boyfriend."

"You guess?"

"Okay, I know." Nico glanced at his feet. "I might not have corrected their assumption. Seemed easier at the time. I didn't know she'd expect my 'boyfriend' to come up for the weekend."

He avoided looking at Luke.

Luke remained quiet for a few beats and then chuckled gruffly.

Nico looked up to Luke running a hand through his hair. "Having let Kent assume you were my boyfriend yesterday, I get it." Luke managed a sheepish smile. "But why don't you tell them you broke up with him?"

"I love them to death, but Nonna likes to meddle in our lives. As the baby of my family, I'm the last one left for her to guide. I'm not interested in dating anyone after Tomas. I just need a break. But if she finds out I'm single, she's going to kick her efforts into high gear, because I need to bring someone to the wedding. That, and I'm getting older now."

"You're getting older, or *she's* getting older?" Luke raised an eyebrow, and boy, if it didn't send heat racing through him. He gritted his teeth against the unneeded attraction.

"Both?" Nico laughed, but Luke had touched on part of the reason. His nonna was getting old, and he just wanted her to see him happy. Even if he had to lie to make it happen.

Nico glanced up at the ceiling. "I shouldn't have asked you."

"You haven't, yet. Exactly." Luke leaned in enough for Nico to catch a hint of citrus and soap and sweat. He gulped in a lungful. "But you should."

A funny thrill raced over Nico's skin, and he straightened, *roommate, jock, this-is-just-a-favor* a mantra in his mind. "Will you pretend to be my boyfriend and come home with me?"

Luke failed to hide a grin and motioned for them to start cleaning. "Tell about me next weekend."

Nico wasn't sure if that was a yes or if Luke needed more details before deciding. "We'd take the train up in the morning, dinner, stay at my parents' Saturday night—you'd have your own room, because . . . well, because."

Luke chuckled. "Because they don't treat you any different than your sister. That's kinda cool."

"Yeah, it is." Nico tried to get a read on what Luke thought, but his expression gave nothing away. "Sunday we'd probably have brunch with the family and then take the train home. I mean, back here."

Funny how he already thought of this as home.

Luke pulled out his phone and scanned it for a few seconds. "Okay, I'm in, but I have a few conditions."

"Conditions? Serious?" The giddy relief was hammered back into a nervous twitch. "What conditions? I didn't ask for conditions before I helped you out."

"Can I help it if you don't know how to negotiate?" Luke was enjoying the moment a little too much. Nico scowled, and Luke chuckled. "If you'd rather I didn't go, just say the word."

Nico growled. "You seriously want to practice extortion with me? *Me*? You're like my Italian padawan that I'm training to be a master. You got nothing on me."

"I don't?" He closed one eye and looked down his nose at Nico.

Nico glared, but felt his lips twitch into a giveaway grin. "Fine. Let me hear your conditions before I say fuhgeddaboudit."

Truth, they'd need to be truly onerous for him to say no.

"First, time permitting, you show me around New York. I've never been."

"Okay, but you realize the city is huge and we're there for less than forty-eight hours."

"Fine, promise to show me around where you live."

Luke sounded serious, but this was hardly a real condition. "Okay."

"Second, I get the window seat on the train. I've never taken a train before."

Also not a real condition. "Really? Sure. I've ridden trains my whole life. You get shotgun."

"Third—"

"Holy fuck. How many conditions do you have?"

"Third." He held up three fingers. "You owe me now."

"Wait." Nico crossed his arms and glared at Luke. "How does that work? This is payback for yesterday."

"Oh, Nico. So naïve." Luke rolled his eyes dramatically. "First, you playing my boyfriend for five minutes is not two full days of pretending. More importantly, you didn't bargain with me first."

"As if. So I was supposed to look at Kurt—"

"Kent," Luke said.

"—and Sebastian and say, hold on, I need to bargain with Luke before I do him a huge solid and pretend to be his boyfriend."

"Hmm." Luke finally dropped his seriously expression. "That's a good point. But this is still way more of a favor than pretending for five minutes."

"Fine. I owe you now."

"Then we have a deal." Luke held out his hand. At least he didn't spit in it first.

They shook, Luke's grip warm and strong, and Nico squeezed into the tremors jumping up his arm. They both let go abruptly, and Nico picked up the sponge.

Luke gently pried the wet sponge free of Nico's grip. "I'll do that, you cooked." He pressed his shoulder against Nico's and pushed gently. Not enough to force him away, but he shifted with it anyway.

"Coffee?" Nico opened the cabinet with the grinds. "Or is that your job too?"

Luke laughed. "It should be, but we'll have it sooner if you do it."

Nico opened the bag and stared inside. The easy way they worked together felt . . . nice. He snuck a peek at Luke. Turning to hide his frown, he scooped coffee into the filter.

Wrong guy, wrong time. But damn, this was going to make it hard to find the *right* guy when the time was right.

CHAPTER EIGHT

Luke

Face plastered to the window, Luke watched as the train slowly exited Philadelphia's 30th Street Station. The inside of the station looked like something out of a movie. Hell, it had probably been used in a ton of films, it was so grand.

Too bad the train wasn't as impressive. The cabin wasn't awful, but he'd hoped for something like the Orient Express. The 8:16 Northeast Regional was just a train. A mostly empty train.

Nico had insisted they get up early to get to New York city sooner so he'd have more time to show Luke around. "Don't want your conditions to go unfulfilled," he'd said.

More like he wanted to torture Luke for haggling over the price of his participation.

He glanced at Nico, who had dressed in tight jeans and a pink button-down shirt. It was the first time since their initial run-in that Luke had seen him in stylish clothes. Nico looked good in them, too. More himself. Comfortable in his own skin.

The change of outfits on the day they left to visit Nico's

family didn't escape Luke's curiosity. Something was going on there.

Something he wanted to understand.

"What?" Nico asked, blinking those devastatingly gorgeous eyes.

Luke shook his head and forced himself to focus on the conductor, gesturing for their tickets.

After they were punched, Nico patted his forearm and led him to the café car.

Talk about underwhelming. By that point, Luke already had low expectations, but this was little more than a vending machine that overcharged by a factor of three. He wanted to kiss Nico for insisting they bring coffee from home, because he wasn't brave enough to try the brown water they were selling. Finally, they settled in for the remaining hour or so to Penn Station.

If he ignored that he had to pretend he was Nico's boyfriend, the idea of seeing New York City excited him. For a country boy from Iowa, this was a big deal. Having Nico to guide him made it so much less daunting.

"You're just like Isaiah." Nico's voice broke Luke's introspective moment.

"Huh?" He turned away from the bland New Jersey suburbs that whizzed by. "How's that?"

"He stared out the window for most of the trip when I took him to New York."

"Do you have a habit of making your roommates pretend to be your boyfriend when you go home?" Luke's amusement faded quickly when his joke landed like an anvil on Nico's head.

"My family never thought he was my boyfriend. I took him to New York for his birthday last year." Nico gave him a weak smile. "He'd never been either."

"Right." Joking about it turned into a total dick move. He hadn't meant it that way. "Sorry, I was just kidding."

"You're fine." It sounded mostly sincere. "Lying to my family doesn't make me feel good. I keep thinking I should just man up and tell them the truth. Then I remember the last time I was home and single, and I can't do it."

"Dare I ask what happened?"

"You can totally ask." Nico sipped, and his eyes glazed over. "Nonna invited Tony Gambrelli to dinner and had the whole family talk me up before they disappeared so we could be alone."

"I take it you and Tony weren't a good match."

"He's a nice guy. We knew each other from around, but neither of us knew what Nonna was up to. And . . ." Nico grimaced. "We'd dated before without our families knowing and it just didn't work."

"Gotcha." Luke refrained from prying. Just.

"With Elliott coming, she'd want to be sure I had a 'plus one' too. Evidently it's embarrassing to be single in my family."

"Understood. But I thought Elliott would ride with us."

"He's flying." Nico opened his iPad. "Dumbass."

"Huh? I thought you liked him."

"I do, but he likes to show off how important he is."

Luke shifted in the roomy seat until he half-faced Nico. "Is he? Important, I mean."

Nico shut the cover and put the tablet down. "I shouldn't have said that. Elliott's family is old money, and the idea of taking a train seemed beneath him."

"So why is he a dumbass?"

"His flight leaves at 10:05 a.m. In order to make that flight, he left about the same time as we did. We'll be at Penn Station about twenty minutes before his flight takes off. These seats are way more comfortable than a commuter plane's—because there is no first class on the short trip from Philly to New York City—and he paid twice what we did for both our tickets combined. Pretty much we'll have less travel time, have a more comfortable trip, arrive before him. All so he can say he flew."

"That does sound stupid."

"Yeah, well. He's not from the city, so he has to learn the hard way." Nico opened his iPad but didn't open the lock screen.

"And what is the 'hard way?'"

"Finding us there before he gets to my parents' house. Commuter planes are noisy and small. I don't recommend them. Plus, he's flying to LaGuardia. It's harder to get to Brooklyn from there than from Penn Station. He probably won't show up before lunch."

Throw in practical to Nico's list of good qualities. "All things being equal, I'm happier taking the train, since I've never been on one."

"Not that I want to diminish your experience, but it isn't that exciting."

"No, but it is my first time—and don't you dare say anything about popping my cherry or how I'm no longer a train virgin."

Nico smirked. "Not that I would say such things, but you're hardly in a position to renegotiate your conditions."

"Whatever." He turned back to the window, trying to act annoyed. Truth was, he and Nico got on way better than he expected. The guy was funny and fun to be with, but he knew when to be serious. Too bad both of them were in a bad place . . .

Yeah, best not to go there.

"This might be a bad time to raise this." Nico didn't sound one ounce concerned it was a bad time. "Did you want to experience the full Monty of railway travel for your first time, or is the train ride enough stimulus for one day?"

Luke laughed. "Full Monty of railway travel? What the hell is that?"

"I'm sure you're aware, I don't live at Penn Station."

"Really? This new learning amazes me. Tell me more."

"Since you asked, the train also doesn't go all the way to my house."

"Shit, there goes my image of this being Amato Railways."

"Seriously, if we owned this business, the café would serve real pastries, not whatever those things with the red stuff in the center sealed in plastic bags were. And coffee that didn't taste like it had been filtered through a train engine."

"You've clearly tried the coffee."

"Hence getting up a few minutes early to make us something drinkable." He raised his reusable mug. "Now that we've establish our train-riding adventure will leave us several miles from our destination, we are left with finding our way to my house. We can take the subway—the full Monty of railway travel—or we can catch an Uber."

"I know you want to get home before your future brother-in-law, so I'll defer to you on this. I wouldn't want to pick the slower route. You wouldn't get to gloat."

"I'm reasonably sure either mode will get us home first, so I'll let you pick. Since I know you like to be in control."

"And you're totally submissive? Not buying that."

"Actually, I'm a switch hitter."

"Really?"

"Yep. Depends on my mood." The color in Nico's cheeks deepened. "TMI?"

"Considering I asked, not sure it could be." Luke winked. "In the spirit of fair play, I switch hit too."

"Um . . . right. Good to know . . . I think." Nico was so adorably flustered, Luke pressed his luck, just to stretch the moment.

"I'm feeling in full Monty mode today, let's take the subway."

"Right." Nico's cheeks flamed. "Just don't give everyone a full Monty on the subway, okay?"

"Of course not." Luke saved that for the right people.

Nico

Nico: We're off the subway. Will be home in ten.

Nonna: Ok, gigio. Looking forward to meeting your bello.

THE TWO-BLOCK WALK HOME NEVER FELT SO short. Bringing Luke along upended him more than anyone else, and it didn't make sense. They weren't really dating, so why did it matter if his family liked Luke?

After a super flirty start to the trip, they'd settled into much calmer conversations. It surprised Nico when the conductor announced Penn Station. Fastest train ride he could remember.

Luke behaved on the subway, though they both snickered when someone said they were enjoying the full New York experience.

"This is my block." He pointed to the Amato's Bakery van parked just ahead of them. "Though that probably gave it away."

"Which one is your house?"

"Um, technically the third and fourth brownstones are my parents' house."

"Third and fourth? Your family owns them both?"

"Yeah, and my grandparents own the next two." Nico opened the gate to let Luke go first. "My great-great-grandfather bought this one first. Over time, my family bought the three next to them."

"Holy shit!" Luke's gaze swept up the front of the house and then moved down the block.

"Just a heads-up." Nico stopped with his key out. "The first floor and the basement are semiconnected to my grandparents' house. The bedrooms are on the second and third floors. People generally wander between the two, so don't be surprised if my grandparents suddenly show up."

"That must take some getting used to."

Nico shrugged and slid the key into the lock. "I guess. This is how it's been since before I was born, so it's all I know."

Nobody was home, at least not in his house. His mother had texted to say his father was at the bakery and she and Elisa had gone out shopping. Nonna, on the other hand, was home.

He led them down a narrow hallway into a formal dining room. They turned right and entered the huge double kitchen the two families shared. Standing in front of the stove, Nonna stirred a pot. She turned when they entered, and the smile split her face.

"Nico!" She wiped her hands on her apron and opened her arms.

Nico put his bag down and bent over to hug his nonna. "You look wonderful."

She kissed him twice before cupping his face and staring at him. "My handsome boy. It's so good to have you home."

It was good to be home. Family meant everything to him, and Nonna was the rock of the family. He covered her hands with his. "I've missed you."

"I always miss you when you're not here. It's not the same without you."

"Maybe soon, I'll be back."

"Maybe?" She wagged her finger at him. "There is no maybe, Nico."

"Yes, Nonna." He grabbed her hand and kissed her fingers. Keeping hold of her, he took a half step back. "Nonna, this is Luke."

"Welcome, Luke. Rosa Marie Amato." She opened her arms, and fortunately Luke went with the moment and let her hug him. "You're taller than I thought you'd be, but that's good since my Nico is so tall."

"Thank you, Mrs. Amato. Nico always smiles when he talks about you, so I'm glad to finally meet you."

Nonna pinched Luke's cheek. "He makes me smile too. Come. Sit. Are you hungry?"

Pulling them both in, she directed them to the table.

"We're good. You promised me peppers and eggs for lunch, so I'm going to wait."

She frowned and shifted her attention to Luke. "You bought one of those awful things on the train, didn't you?"

"No, ma'am. Nico warned me not to try them."

"We ate before we left Philadelphia, and before we got on the subway we split a bagel."

"Better than train food . . . barely." She picked up a wooden spoon and returned to the stove. "Go put your bags away and come back. I just put the coffee on. It will be done soon."

"Sure." Nico stood and nodded back the way they'd come. "Did Mama say which room she put Luke in?"

Nonna turned and eyed them both for a second. "Luke is staying in the guest room next to yours."

"Great. Be back in a few minutes." He snagged the straps to his bag and hustled Luke out of the kitchen.

Luke

Coury: How's the visit with your fake boyfriend's family?

Luke: STFU.

Coury: What? Why you hating on me? Seriously, how's it going?

Luke: It's going.

LUKE PUSHED his phone into his pocket, still burning with embarrassment. Embarrassment even the fresh garden air couldn't lessen. He slumped onto a wooden bench and ground his palms against his forehead.

He'd tried to engage in the family conversation over dinner, but how was he supposed to know Nico's family pronounced marinara, "madanad?" Or that calling it pasta sauce was borderline insulting to his grandmother? And what the hell was gabagool? Even Elliott knew the right way to say things in the Amato house, and he wasn't an ounce Italian.

"Hey." Nico shut the back door and sat next to Luke, handing him a glass of wine. "Here. It's a full-bodied zinfandel."

"Thanks." More cluelessness. What made the wine full-bodied? "Sorry."

"For what?" Nico set his drink down and gently rubbed Luke's back. "I thought things went well."

The smooth motion soothed some of Luke's anxiety. He leaned into the massage.

"Clearly I didn't study the right things."

Nico's hand paused on his back. "You studied to come here?"

"Just food stuff. I didn't want to sound stupid."

Nico's hand drifted up and kneaded the tight muscles in Luke's neck. "That's . . . really considerate of you. Thank you."

Luke tasted his wine, and Nico removed his hand. Once gone, Luke missed the contact. Not that he could ask Nico to keep doing it. "Yeah, well it didn't help. I still looked stupid, and your family thinks I'm an idiot."

"Actually, they really like you."

"You don't have to be nice."

"No, really. If they didn't like you, you'd know it. Elisa brought home this total dickwad once. Five minutes into dinner, Papà and Nonno started talking smack about him in Italian. Nonna called him a jackass, which is about the second-worst curse word she uses."

"What did your sister say when this was happening?"

"I think she was more embarrassed by the guy than by the family. Even she could tell he was being a jackass." Nico picked up his glass. "You, however, were great."

"Right."

"I'm serious. You were respectful, but not too meek. You didn't try to turn any conversation onto yourself, and you offered to help clear the table. That alone earned you Nonna's seal of approval."

"Now I know you're lying. She almost stabbed me with her fork when I offered."

Nico snorted. "I saw that. But it's not what you think. Guests don't help."

"Elliott helped."

"Yeah, but he's about to marry my sister. If you kept coming home with me, then they'd expect you to help." Nico bit his lip, frowned, and stared into the yard. "But I promise I won't foist this craziness on you again."

The finality of Nico's promise filled Luke with . . . something. Regret came closest. "It's all good. Your family's great."

"They are great, and I love them to death."

"But?"

Nico eyed the back door and leaned in to whisper, "Sometimes they're a bit much."

Luke laughed. "That's all families." He bumped his shoulder against Nico's. When Nico pushed back, Luke didn't move.

They sat, pressed together, staring out at the yard.

Fake boyfriends. Fake boyfriends. *Fake.*

Nico had made it clear he wasn't ready to date, let alone have a boyfriend.

Besides, Luke wasn't in the right place to date either. So why did it feel like jolts of electricity kept zapping between them? And why, when the conversation inside had gotten lively, had Luke felt warm and heavy? Like *he* was with family.

A burst of laughter made them both turn toward the house. "Something's funny," Luke said.

Nico finished his wine, arm shifting from Luke's, and Luke felt the loss.

"Work, children, or neighbors. It has to be one of those topics. If I had to guess, it would be kids. Probably my brother Joey sent a picture of his kids doing something silly."

"Are you and your brother close?"

"Sorta yes and sorta no." Nico tucked his right leg under his ass and turned toward Luke. "He's ten years older than me. I was eight the last time we spent more than a few days together. There weren't a lot of shared interests during those years."

Luke snorted. "I can see how that'd happen."

"Then he went to college in California, met his wife, went to med school, had children, and in general began adulting way before I was ready to join him. Joey always made time for me when he was home, and I love him to death, but we never had the time Elisa and I did."

"You miss him."

Nico smiled. "Missed having him when he left."

"Did you tell him?"

"No," he said softly. "Joey needed to fly off. He loves us, but what you see inside tends to overwhelm him. I was really mad at him when he left. When I got older, Nonna told me he didn't want to leave me and Elisa, but he needed to go away to find himself."

"Having left Iowa to do the same, I understand."

A sad smile appeared, and Nico seemed far away. "He never wanted to be a baker. Didn't want to live in this family compound surrounded by generations. He didn't want his kids to feel the weight of expectations he didn't want to embrace. Everyone understands, and no one is mad at him for leaving. Well, no one other than his eight-year-old brother."

"Not his twenty-one-year-old brother?"

"Nope. I'm happy for him." Nico returned his gaze to Luke. "But I miss him."

"I get it."

Nico stirred on the bench and rubbed his jaw. "This might not be the best time to share this, but I got an email from Amazon about the air mattress."

Luke's stomach lurched. "And?"

"It was damaged in shipping and they cancelled the order, but I'm free to reorder it."

A laugh bubbled out of Luke. "Ugh! They did that to me once. Said that because a third party sold it, they didn't automatically ship a new one."

"Exactly, which is some bullshit." Nico took a deep breath and blew it out. "I'll order a new one tonight, and I'll pay for the express shipping this time."

"You don't need to do that." Luke clapped his mouth shut. "I mean, why spend the extra money? Sharing a bed hasn't been an issue. Has it?"

Nico glanced down at their feet and then looked up at Luke, almost shyly. "No, you've been a perfect gentleman."

"So save the money."

"I won't order until tomorrow, so if you change your mind, let me know."

"You betcha. But I won't."

Nico shoulder-bumped him, their arms settling together—

The back door opened, and they jerked apart.

"Hey, guys," Elisa said, face rosy from wine. "Dessert is ready."

"Thanks, E. We're coming in." Nico grabbed his wineglass.

He couldn't tell for sure, but Nico appeared to adjust himself before moving from the bench. That he kept his back to Luke was good: it gave Luke time to do the same.

AFTER ANOTHER GLASS OF THE "FULL-BODIED" zinfandel and dessert, Luke sat in an armchair and basked in the merry buzz thrumming through his veins.

Dinner had been nice. Nicer was how Nico watched out for

him, stopping his father from serving Luke a second glass of port. "He's not used to this much wine, Papà," he'd said. "Too much of this might make him sick."

Someone clomped down the stairs. Had to be Nico. Everyone else said they were going to sleep. Bakers' hours, Nico's father said as he shook Luke's hand.

Luke felt Nico's presence prickle at his side and opened his eyes.

"Hey." Nico grinned and set a glass of water on the table beside him. "Helps prevent hangovers."

"I didn't drink *that* much."

"Port is notorious for giving hangovers." Nico drained a third of his own glass.

Luke followed the example. "I have a question. A couple, actually."

"Hopefully, I have good answers."

He tried to give Nico what Nonna called the stink eye. "Right, because any old answer wouldn't do."

"I'm not the one who prefaced things with, 'I have a question.' Did you think I wouldn't realize you were asking me something?"

"Remind me again why I came here?"

Nico snorted and perched on the arm of Luke's chair. "Because you are one of the nicest guys on the planet and you didn't want to see me suffer."

Maybe it was the buzz playing tricks on him, but it didn't sound like Nico was being sarcastic. "Right, not like I owed you or nothing."

"If you *really* felt obligated, you'd have said no when I asked." He toasted Luke with his water. Their glasses dinged. "You're a good friend."

Luke sucked in a deep breath. Friend. Yeah. Yeah, he liked the label.

So what if they'd only known each other a couple of weeks?

Luke had never been so in tune with someone before. So comfortable.

Friend.

Friend.

Nico licked a drop of water from his finger, and Luke dropped his gaze resolutely to his glass. "What's your first question, Luke?"

Luke rubbed the rim of his glass with his thumb and looked over at Nico's pink shirt and tight—Christ, *so* tight—jeans. "You dressed different today." *Better.*

A moment of silence stretched the air between them. "Was that supposed to be a question? Perhaps you need to revisit first grade English?"

"I mean, you're dressed like the first couple of times I saw you."

"Still not a question."

"Why?"

Nico shrugged, and for one awful second Luke thought he'd get off the arm of the chair and force more distance between them. A tight laugh left Nico. One Luke didn't trust a bit. "Nonna thinks I should dress nicer when we have company for dinner."

Luke didn't believe Nico for a second, but he also felt Nico's resistance to talk about it. "Gotcha."

He'd piece together the mystery another time.

"What's your other question?" Nico asked.

Luke took another gulp of water. "What was up with all that tapping the glasses with knives?"

Nico squirmed on the arm of the chair. "Ah, that. Practice."

"Practice? Does your family do the carol of the wine glasses instead of bells at Christmas?"

"You're *so* not a real Italian." Nico twisted so he faced Luke. "At Italian weddings—and major milestone anniversary parties, too—when someone wants the bride and groom to kiss, they tap their knife to the wineglass. If everyone joins in, the couple of the day has to oblige. Once they kiss, all the happy couples are supposed to join in."

"And if a couple doesn't kiss?"

"The rest of the family gossips about how they're on the rocks." Nico fanned his hands on his chest, mimicking the drama. "Did you see so-and-so? They *didn't* kiss after the bride and groom. I bet there's infidelity going on. Do you think she's schtupping the bakery guy?"

"Schtupping? You made that up."

Nico stared at him blankly. Finally, he shook his head, lips twitching. "No, I didn't, but clearly civilization stops at the Mississippi river. It's another word for shagging, bumping uglies, the mattress mambo, or if none of those ring a bell, *fucking*."

Luke reached over Nico and set his glass on the table. The proximity of Luke's arm over Nico's warm lap had Nico tensing and Luke hurriedly pulled back. "So if a couple doesn't kiss, your family will think there's trouble in paradise?"

"It's all talk. The older generation needs something scandalous to keep their blood moving." He shrugged. "Nonno thinks it's funny to make E and Elliott practice whenever they're over for dinner."

"And your parents and grandparents followed their lead."

"Every time."

"And we didn't."

Nico blinked rapidly, then he held up a finger. "Ah, right. No, we didn't, but no one really expected us to."

"Because . . .? Do they think we're schtupping other people?"

Nico laughed so hard, he dropped into the armchair with Luke. He immediately apologized and shifted, and Luke grabbed his arm, keeping him on the cushion.

Nico glanced down at Luke's hand and swallowed. "They don't expect us to join in because you're not well-versed in our family traditions."

Luke's blood thrummed until he could hear his heart in his

ears. It was the wine. It was Nico, making him feel like he stood on a live wire. He lowered his voice. "But I am now."

"Hmm?" Nico wriggled next to him, like he was torn between jumping to his feet and twisting his body to face Luke's.

"Will they do this again at brunch tomorrow?"

"I would think so. Yeah."

"Which means they'll assume I know what it means, and by our not kissing, they'll figure out we're not really dating."

Nico sucked air through his teeth and avoided looking at Luke. "I doubt it. We haven't been 'dating' long enough for it to apply to us. And besides," he flashed Luke a grin, "I need to come clean at some point. If this makes them ask, it'll be a good time to tell them the truth."

In their almost two weeks together, Luke had realized Nico hid his emotions well—until you knew him better. Usually it was a small change in facial expression followed by an over-compensating smile. This mattered to Nico. He might think he should tell his family they weren't dating, but he didn't *want* to tell them.

The flush on Nico's cheeks deepened.

Luke lifted a hand to Nico's chin and steered his face around. Nico's eyes were dark and glittery, and his lips parted—

Luke leaned forward and kissed him. Soft, at first. A question. Their breaths tangled, and Nico didn't turn away.

Luke clasped the back of Nico's neck and pressed their lips together again. A little moan slipped out of Nico, and the sound rippled shivers through Luke. He darted his tongue over Nico's bottom lip—

Nico pulled back suddenly, whispering, "What are we doing?"

"Practicing."

"Practicing?"

"When your family starts tapping wineglasses tomorrow, I don't want it to be the first time we've kissed. It'll be a dead give-away. So . . . practice."

Nico gnawed his lip as he processed the explanation. A small smile pulled at his lips. "Practice."

Luke tilted forward. "Practice."

Their lips met again, and Nico's parted, inviting Luke to deepen the kiss.

A practice kiss. *Fake.*

But that didn't stop Luke's heart hammering at the feeling of Nico's tongue sliding against his own. Didn't stop him tasting the trace of sweet port and melting at Nico's low groan. Didn't stop his dick from getting fired up.

Nico returned the kiss, matching Luke for every thrust of his tongue. His hand slid around Luke's waist, the warmth of his gripping fingers soaking into him.

Nico kissed Luke like he enjoyed what he was doing. If Luke ranked all the things he wanted from a boyfriend, a good kisser would be near the top. Kent had failed that requirement. He'd never seemed to like kissing. Never leaned into it as passionately as Nico was doing.

God, that was a huge turn-on. Of course his *fake* boyfriend had to tick that box.

Fake. Dammit. This couldn't go on forever—no matter how easy it was. He was kissing Nico so they wouldn't be awkward at brunch tomorrow. So they'd keep Nico's nonna happy.

That was all.

That. Was. All.

CHAPTER NINE

Nico

Elisa: OMG, boo! I love it. So much better than the one she picked.

Nico: She didn't know you like I do.

Elisa: This plus the flowers! You're the best!

Nico: Just doing my job.

"Really?" Nico almost dropped the phone trying to access his calendar. "Sure, I can be there tomorrow at ten."

Pen in hand, he grabbed a napkin and wrote down the name he'd been given. When he finished, he nodded. What a dork. Mrs. Esposito couldn't see him over the phone. "Yes, got it. Thank you."

He disconnected the call and tossed the phone on the couch. This was good. Well, he thought it was good. Elisa would complain, and Papà would ask—only half joking—why he was paying Nico.

"This calls for a celebration." Saying that to an empty apartment killed the euphoria. "Or a run."

Two plus weeks into his stint as a wedding planner, he'd finished most of his to-do list. Things would pick up the week before the wedding, but that was weeks away. He was getting bored.

Glancing at the clock on the microwave, he waffled on the run. His and Luke's first two days back from New York, Luke had worked late. And texted Nico both times. It was very considerate, but also a bit curious. Had their fake kissing made Luke leery of coming home?

Was he embarrassed by the way Nico's family had oohhed and ahhed over their short but electric kiss at brunch? He'd felt Luke tremble beside him after they were done and had clasped a steadying hand on his knee under the table.

Just a friendly squeeze. Just to say *thanks* and *are you okay*?

Luke had been the one to thread his fingers over Nico's and place their joined hands on the table where all the family could see. Luke had been the one to kiss him in front of his family again before they left for the train . . .

But maybe, that weekend behind them, Luke felt silly how into the fake thing he'd gotten?

Nico sighed, tried not to recall the delicious pressure of Luke's lips against his own.

He changed and stretched. If Luke didn't stay late or go out with coworkers, he'd be home soon. Nico could start cooking then. Otherwise, he'd go for a run and make dinner when he got back.

Sitting on the living room floor, he reached forward until he felt it in his hamstrings. He'd switched legs twice and was about to do the right leg the second time when Luke popped through the front door. He jumped when he saw Nico on the floor.

"Crap, you scared me."

"I have that effect on people." Nico leaned into his stretch without looking up.

"I'd ask the obvious, but I assume you're going for a run?" Luke walked past him and into their bedroom.

"I wasn't sure when you'd be home tonight." He stood and loosened up his quads. "Now that you're here, I'll make dinner."

His tie gone, Luke stepped into the common room, unbuttoning his white dress shirt. "So you *do* wait for me to make dinner."

Nico stared at the slip of threadbare undershirt that did little to hide Luke's defined chest. "Huh? Oh." Nico pulled his gaze to Luke's face, forcing himself to shrug nonchalantly. "I told you I don't like eating alone."

"Me neither. Do you mind waiting? I'd love to go running with you."

"You want to run with me?"

"Why do you sound so skeptical? Afraid I'll smoke you?"

The smug jock-boy look on Luke's face reminded Nico why he preferred running alone. "Please. I've been running since I was ten. Even after soccer, I kept up my training. Maybe I'm skeptical because I don't want you to slow me down?"

"Ouch." Luke grimaced. "I totally deserved that, didn't I?"

"And more. Get changed, stretch, and we'll see who smokes whom."

NICO OPENED THEIR DOOR, flushed from the exercise.

They'd stayed pretty much even, but Nico had been running every day since they arrived. Luke hadn't been since he left Harrison and had ended a bit winded. Still, they ran well together, and Nico enjoyed it more than usual.

"I thought I'd make macaroni and use the last of Nonna's

gravy." Nico didn't wait for an answer before detouring into the kitchen.

"Translation: pasta and pasta sauce." Luke seemed proud of himself.

"That's what I said. I didn't say madanad, because I remember how that confused you."

"That's because it's a made-up word."

"Only to those not from New York." Luke was right, but Nico had grown up hearing everyone use the word instead of marinara.

"Nope, I looked it up. Even the New York Italian-American websites say it's bullshit. I believe the quote was 'just because everyone knows what you mean, doesn't mean it's a real word.'"

"Fine, we're having *pasta* and *mar-in-ara.* Happy?"

"Oh, you sound so sexy when you talk like that." Luke leaned back and fanned himself with his hand. "Say it again?"

"Whatever." Nico opened the refrigerator for the *madanad.* "If you want, you can shower while I cook."

"Hardly seems fair that I shower first." Luke pulled out two tall glasses and then got the pitcher of water from the refrigerator. "We should do it together."

Nico nearly dropped the container of sauce. The image of them naked under the spray popped into his head, and his dick was *real* interested.

He faced the oven, biting the inside of his cheek. "Thanks for the offer, but I don't think there's room in that shower for us both."

Luke sprayed water over Nico's face and neck. Plucking two paper towels, Nico wiped his face.

"Sorry," Luke said, lips wobbling on a laugh. "I meant we should make dinner together."

"Oh, my bad." Nico fanned his face like Luke had done. "I thought you were still pretending I was sexy. I played along."

Luke let a belly laugh ring out, closing his eyes, hands waving about.

Nico smiled tightly. This was why he shouldn't let any feelings grow between them. Luke was just like any other jock in the end, and while they might get on okay as friends, while they might even have this weirdly kinetic connection, nothing substantial would last between them.

"God." Luke took another sip of water and choked as another laugh broke free.

Luke coughed and spluttered, and Nico sighed.

"Look up." He demonstrated. "That's what my mother always tells me."

Luke did as suggested, and a few seconds later he regained control. "I'll be dipped. That works."

"Glad I could help," Nico said, fighting not to scowl. He *was* sexy, thank you very much.

"Cough aside, I needed that laugh."

Nico turned the burner on low and slammed the cover on the pan. He'd make sure his next boyfriend, whoever that was, would appreciate the fact.

He bit down on speaking his mind and did what he did best. Shrugged it off. Pretended it didn't hurt. "Why? Bad day?"

Luke frowned, then seemed to shake it off. "Not really." He put a big pot under the tap and filled it.

"Which means yes. What's wrong?"

"Honestly, there's nothing *wrong*." Luke transferred the pot to the stove. He looked at Nico, eyes still glittering from his laugh. The smile seemed warm and genuine and a little shy, but Nico didn't want to read into it.

Luke hesitated. "We'll take turns showering and I'll tell you about it, yeah?"

Nico shrugged and slung off a "Sure," annoyed at himself that he really wanted to know.

Luke

Kent: Are you bringing Nero?

Luke: Only if you bring Sylvester.

Kent: Don't be an asshole.

Luke: Good advice. Follow it.

LUKE SHOULD BLOCK the dickhead already. Why did Kent even care what Luke did? Better question, why did Luke bother to respond?

The shower cut off, and he stuffed his phone in his pocket. Luke wanted dinner ready when Nico came out. Not that he did any real cooking. Nonna had made the sauce, and even Luke could boil pasta. He tossed in the penne and set the timer—per the instructions Nico left. Which meant it *really* wasn't like he cooked.

The phone vibrated in his pocket, but Luke refused to check. Nico always knew when Kent sent a message. It wasn't hard to figure out when Luke scowled at his phone.

He wouldn't let his ex ruin another night. Especially not tonight. Nico might get the wrong idea.

"How's dinner coming?" Nico ran his hands across his wet hair.

Luke couldn't deny how super hot it was. "The *macaroni* is cooking and the *madanad* should be warm enough."

"Excellent." Nico used the wooden spoon to stir the sauce. "When I was a kid, my family used all these slang words for regular stuff. Madanad, mutzadel for mozzarella, riguta for ricotta cheese. I thought they were real."

"Right. So, what's gabagool?"

Nico shrugged, looking sheepish. "Capicola."

"Seriously? How do you get gabagool from that?"

"No idea." He tapped the spoon on the edge of the pot and set it down. "When I was about sixteen, we went to the Jersey Shore for a week during the summer. I tried to be helpful and went shopping at the Acme, the local grocery store. I stared at the deli counter for like five minutes until the guy asks me if I'm looking for something specific.

"I say, 'yes, I'd like a half a pound of brahjzoot sliced thin.'"

Luke snorted. "What the hell is that?"

"You heard the guy, eh?" Nico winked and set the strainer in the sink. "Brahjzoot is what my family calls prosciutto."

"The fuck?"

"Exactly. I never knew the correct name was prosciutto. Sixteen and I was still calling things by these weird-ass names people in my community used instead of the real thing. The funny thing is, if you go to any deli in New York and ask for brahjzoot or gabagool, you'll get prosciutto or capicola."

"That's . . ." Bizarre, and oddly adorable.

"Fucked-up?" Nico nodded. "You can say it."

Luke could say it. But could he say the adorable bit?

"I feel like my family trained me to speak a weird language no one understands so I couldn't leave the neighborhood."

Luke snorted, relieved Nico had moved on so he didn't have to speak.

He loved Nico's stories. Found it fascinating how easily Nico slid between two worlds. More so than his parents and grandparents, it seemed.

When the pasta was finished, Nico pulled out a loaf of Italian bread and made them plates. They both sat, and Luke paused. It felt nice, eating good food at home with someone to banter with.

"So, what happened today? Or have you decided you'd rather not talk about it?" Nico didn't look up as he sprinkled grated cheese on his pasta. When he finished, he offered the cannister to Luke, who took it, hesitating again.

"Nothing bad, really." Luke shoveled food into his mouth to buy himself some time.

Nico saw right through that, judging by his arched brow.

Luke swallowed and dropped his fork onto the plate. "The firm holds these events for their interns all summer. The last two nights, they had receptions with key clients. Those were more workish. Saturday, they're having a thing at the Phillies game."

"That's what has you all wonky?" Nico broke off a piece of bread and ran it through the sauce in his bowl. "You love baseball. Why isn't a free game a 'hell yeah' moment? Or is it not free?"

"No, it's free. They don't make us pay for anything. They have a luxury box they're using."

"Nice. I got invited to one at Citi Field for a Mets game. Swanky." He speared more pasta and continued to eat.

"It's a plus one event."

"Really? They're making you bring someone?"

"Not making us, but they made it clear this event welcomed significant others." Why was he dancing around the issue? Nico wasn't stupid, he'd figure it out. He needed to man up. "I wanted to know . . . would you be interested? In going with me?"

Nico's gaze shot to his, something glistening in his eyes, but he blinked before Luke got a read. Nico dragged his fork through his dinner, head cocked to the side in thought. "Calling in your fake-boyfriend favor?"

Luke's stomach flipped. "Sorta. I mean, if you don't want to go, I understand."

Nico didn't answer immediately, which should have been enough for Luke to tell Nico it wasn't important. Forget it.

Problem was, Luke didn't *want* to tell Nico that.

"I have a question before I agree."

Luke shifted nervously on his chair. "Shoot."

"It doesn't sound like you *have* to take someone, and it's not like I'm a huge baseball fan." Nico raised an eyebrow. "What's the real reason you're asking?"

Luke pushed his food away. Part of the reason made him look petty. What did it matter what Kent thought? Even if Nico didn't go, Luke could still pretend he had an adoring boyfriend who *didn't think he was boring in the slightest*.

He didn't *need* Nico to come. He *wanted* him there. Really wanted him there. "I'd rather not go alone."

"Because of Kent." Nico cut through the bullshit, but his expression was unreadable.

Luke hated the stodgy feeling in his gut. Like maybe he was disappointing Nico.

"Not just to pretend I found someone new," he rushed out. "He's the only person I know. If I go by myself, I have to choose between talking to him and his new boyfriend, or being alone most of the time. And," Luke looked over the table at him, "I like hanging out with you."

Nico held his gaze for a moment before refocusing on his pasta. "You don't care that I'm a baseball dunce?"

"Nope. I'll gladly explain anything you don't understand."

"Even if I ask why there isn't a coin flip before overtime?"

There it was again. Enough confidence in himself to poke fun at his past mistakes. Admirable. "Especially then."

"Okay, I'm in."

"Really? That's awesome. I totally owe you."

"Yep, you totally do." Nico's smirk didn't bode well. "And with that, I have something to tell you."

Was he serious? They hadn't even gone to the game, and he was calling in the favor? "Why am I scared?" Why was his pulse beating so hard and his palms sweating?

"Because you think I'll tell you what I demand in return for attending a baseball game. Nico exaggerated a shudder. "But you're wrong." He snapped a finger at Luke and returned to his dinner.

Luke waited, but Nico didn't continue. After a couple of seconds, he pulled his plate closer. "*And?*"

Nico peered over the fork. "Not scared anymore?"

"Petrified." The aroma of the *madanad* called back his appetite. He took another delicious bite.

"I have a part-time job."

Luke jerked his head up to Nico, grinning. "What?

"A part-time job." Nico preened liked he'd been elected king of the prom. "I told you I didn't have enough to keep me busy."

"Right, but you said no one would hire you for just a few weeks."

"I was wrong. Someone did."

Nico was skimping on the details on purpose. Two could play that game. "That's great. I hope it works out for you." Luke bit into his bread.

Nico glared at him. "You're such a brat."

"Me?" He sprayed bits of food onto the table. Putting his hand in front of his mouth, he added, "You were the one being coy."

"Only because you thought the worst of me."

Luke laughed. "You have to admit, the timing *was* really suggestive."

"I admit to nothing, Mr. DeRosa." Nico took a dramatic bite from his bread.

"Then continue to be delusional and dramatic, Mr. Amato." Luke stuffed his fork into the pasta and chomped on the contents.

Nico's mood flattened. He plastered on a smile, and Luke knew he'd fucked up. Said something wrong. Did he take offense to Luke's joke?

Luke leaned back in his chair and studied Nico. Since their trip to New York, he'd returned to dressing in plain clothes. Cargo shorts and T-shirts mainly. Tonight was no exception.

The mystery was slowly solving itself, and the truth of it made Luke ache. He rubbed his jaw, unsure what to say. Whether he should say anything at all.

"I'm working at Esposito's," Nico said, and Luke put away his revelation to study later.

He flashed a grin at Nico. "You *are* working for the enemy?"

Nico rolled his eyes and raised his hand as if to gesture but dropped it quickly into his lap.

Luke swallowed hard.

"They're not the enemy," Nico said. "I hired them to make Elisa's wedding cake. After I mentioned to Mrs. Esposito I was running out of things to do, she asked if I wanted to work a few hours a day there. I mean, I won't earn much, but it's not entirely about the money."

"Did you tell your family yet?"

Nico rolled his eyes. "Har-har. I did, but Rocco Esposito and my dad know each other from trade shows and the like. Rocco called my dad before he offered me a job to be sure Papà would be okay with me working for him."

"Cool. What are you hours?"

"Don't worry, I'll be home in time to cook." He winked. Luke hoped Nico knew he never expected that. "They'll vary. Mostly I'm filling in for people or providing extra coverage during busy times, like morning rush or lunch. Maybe a weekend morning, but Estelle said they have plenty of part-timers available weekend mornings, so probably not."

"Sounds pretty perfect." Especially the part where Nico's weekends would be mostly free.

"It does. And it won't interfere with the game you're so eager to show me off at." He gave Luke a stink eye Nonna would be proud of. "Still worried?"

"Nope."

Yes.

But for entirely different reasons.

CHAPTER TEN

Nico

Nico: Be proud of me, I'm going to a baseball game today.

Isaiah: Sitting in a luxury box isn't really going to a game.

Nico: Don't be spiteful because I'm finally doing something your filthy-rich, super-sweet boyfriend usually does for you.

Isaiah: Whatever. Just don't forget the event at Darren's house in two weeks.

Right, the charity fundraiser Darren's mother sponsored. Isaiah must truly be in love to agree to play for that event.

It would be great to see Isaiah again, even if he would hassle him for more details of this fake boyfriend thing he had going with Luke.

He'd cross that bridge when he got to it.

First, he needed to deal with today.

He'd searched for a good 'baseball for beginners' website and found a couple that helped. The infield fly rule was pretty straightforward, and stealing bases made sense, but what the fuck was a balk? And who came up with the number system? The shortstop and second baseman stood in about the same place, on opposite sides of second base. So why did they designate the second baseman number four, skip the shortstop, and make the third baseman number five, then go back to the shortstop as number six? Ugh, it made no sense.

He didn't realize Luke had come into the common room until he saw a pair of legs standing next to him. A pair of well-muscled, nicely hairy legs in skimpy soccer shorts.

"What are you doing?" Luke peered over Nico's laptop, and Nico hurriedly started to shut it.

"Just reading something."

Luke pinched the screen still. "Baseball for Dummies?" The gently amused look froze Nico. "What are you up to?"

"Nothing." He steered the laptop screen out of Luke's sight. "I was reading about baseball."

"I see that. Why?"

"Because . . ." He glared at the screen and looked up. "I don't want to say something stupid like 'how many points did they get' or 'why isn't that a yellow card?'"

"Nico." Luke squatted until he was at eye level. "One of the things I like most about you is that you're not afraid to be who you are. I wish I had your self-confidence."

"I'm not as self-confident as you think."

Luke's gaze momentarily dropped to his simple white T-shirt and jumped back to his eyes again. "It's a company outing, not a baseball writers convention. Most people won't know the difference between a pass ball and a wild pitch."

"Catcher mistake versus pitcher's."

Luke raised an eyebrow. "Impressive. Look, you don't need to worry. Most of the people are going to see and be seen." He paused a second before adding, "And to get free food and drink."

"But *you're* going because you're interested in the game, too." And Nico was his plus one. He wouldn't be much of a companion if he didn't get the game.

He rubbed his palm nervously over the arm of the couch.

Luke rested a warm hand on top of Nico's, stilling him. "Thank you." He pushed himself to his feet. "But I think you know enough. We should get going soon, and you need to shower."

"What?" Nico sniffed his armpit. "I poured water over my head during our run."

Luke pried the laptop free, set it aside, and pulled Nico to his feet, grinning. "And that wore off an hour ago. Jump in the shower while I figure out how we get there using SEPTA."

THE LUXURY SUITE at Citizens Bank Park didn't disappoint. It had indoor and outdoor seating separated by sliding glass panels, a bar, a buffet, barstools and tables, three TVs, and several couch-like seats.

Two servers walked around with food, one of whom was totally hot. Nothing compared to Luke—let's just be honest here—but gazing at the waiter was more appropriate than gazing at Luke. Even if he should be playing it up as his plus-one fake boyfriend.

It just . . . it didn't *feel* very fake, and that was frying Nico's synapses. Screwing with his resolve not to crush on another jock.

Fuck. Focus on the moment. On the suite. He looked around. Not quite as nice as the one at CitiField in New York. And not just because he was from New York either. The . . . well, those . . . actually, it was just as nice. But definitely not *nicer*.

The glass panels were closed today, given the temperature, but

Nico slid them open and slipped outside. Luke's partner wanted to introduce him to the senior people, and Nico knew enough to let that happen without him.

Kent and Sebastian had just shown up—three innings into the game—and Kent immediately showed off his very important boyfriend. The pained look on Sebastian's face made Nico feel for the guy. Sebastian probably didn't know the score with Kent, or maybe he was starting to suspect. Someone should tell him. Just not Nico. That could never come off well.

Only two other people sat outside, and they sat in the first two seats of the front row. Figuring others would soon come out, Nico sat at the far end.

The game was uneventful, but still good. Aaron Nola, the Phillies' best pitcher, mowed down the Chicago Cubs. He was working on a shutout. That fact Nico knew what that meant gave him a twinge of pride. *Go, me!*

One of the Phillies hit a high fly deep to the left field side. The crowd stood and cheered, until the outfielder caught it for the third out. Nico needed a drink but stopped when Kent walked toward him.

"Hi, Nino." There was just enough snark in his voice that Nico knew the slipup had been intentional.

Kent held out his hand as he closed the last few feet.

Several thoughts raced through Nico's mind: ignore the offered shake, spit in his hand before accepting, squeeze Kent's hand as hard as he could, or . . .

Nico flashed his dimples and pumped Kent's hand. "Kirk, how are you?"

"It's Kent."

"I know." He jerked his hand back, still smiling. "Just like *you* know my name is Nico."

Kent's lips thinned, and his jaw muscles twitched. When Nico tried to walk around him, Kent didn't budge, effectively blocking the way. "You're not that big a deal, you know."

"Says the nobody trying to block me from getting a drink." Shaking his head, Nico stepped over his chair into the row above.

"Oh right, the mighty Amato bakery boy. Yes, I'm sure everyone here is so impressed."

Nico stopped, looked at Kent for a moment and then inside where Sebastian talked to Luke and Luke's mentor.

Nico kept his voice low. "You scummy piece of shit. You cheated on Luke, left him in a financial bind, and broke his heart just so you could leverage Sebastian's family into a job offer. I've seen my fair share of snakes in my time, but you are one of the biggest."

"You don't know shit, dough boy." Kent hopped the row, cramming his face in front of Nico's. "Luke's a fool. He's so straitlaced, he'll never get ahead. His career goals are to become Mr. Salaryman. To settle down and plan for the future. Boring. That's not for me."

"Fine, he's not for you, but that justified cheating on him? Pretending you'd help pay for the apartment you knew he couldn't afford on his own?" Nico leaned in, making sure to use his height to look down at Kent. "You're a user. Nonna calls people like you *porca troia*. And you are. Now, please step aside."

The outer door opened, and Luke stepped out holding two glasses of wine. His dark eyes landed on them warily. Kent followed Nico's gaze and inched back.

"Nice talking to you, Nico." The fake smile made Nico's skin itch. "I need to get back to Seb."

Nico forced himself to smile and waved at Kent. "Good talking to you too."

"Sebastian is getting you a drink," Luke said to Kent. Clearly, he hadn't heard their conversation. "Said he'd meet us here."

"Great." Kent glanced at Nico. "I'll find him, and we'll be right out."

Nico filled his cheeks with air and slowly exhaled.

"What was that about?" He handed Nico a glass. "I have no

idea if it's *full-bodied,* but Mr. Rayner said the riesling was good, so I got two."

"I see your boss likes sweet things." Nico smirked before he took a sip. "But he's right, this is good."

Luke tasted his wine. "And you're right, it is sweet. What were you and Kent talking about?"

"Not much." He didn't like lying, but Luke obviously wasn't hating on his ex. "He mentioned his future plans. How he wants to get hired after the summer."

Luke snorted. "That would explain the beeline to Mr. Rayner when they arrived. He interrupted us in his hurry to introduce Sebastian Forsythe."

"How'd that go?" Not that he cared. Careful not to spill his drink, Nico stepped down and sat in the seat he'd been using before.

"Probably not as well as Kent was hoping. Mr. Rayner shook hands, then continued our conversation. Kent said something about seeing if you wanted a drink and left Seb with us."

"That was . . ." *Shitty of him.* "Nice of him to think of me."

"He took off before I could tell him I was going to get you something." Luke took another drink. "It didn't look like you two were discussing future plans."

From the corner of his eye, Nico saw Luke look at him. He tried to feign interest in the game, but he couldn't keep it up. "I told him you deserved much better than how he treated you. He told me I didn't know what I was talking about. We agreed to disagree when you showed up."

Luke watched him for a long moment, then leaned over and feathered a kiss on Nico's cheek. "Thank you."

"It's true." Nico put his hand on his cheek, feeling the warm ghost of Luke's lips. "Your next boyfriend needs to treat you right. If you like . . ."

"Yeah?"

"If you like, when we're done pretending to be boyfriends, you can let me . . . you know, tell you if they're doing right by you." He'd nearly slipped and offered to show him how he should be treated. But he wasn't the one Luke wanted.

Even if Luke was vaguely curious about them, Nico hadn't been acting one hundred percent himself. And as soon as he did, Luke would lose any interest. He'd be the Luke he'd first encountered at Harrison. Maybe a little less douchey, because they were friends.

Friends, and *fake* boyfriends.

He dropped his hand from his cheek.

Luke's smile wavered, and he quickly took a drink. "Thanks, but I think I need to figure out who is treating me right on my own, if you know what I mean."

"Yeah, I do."

Luke put his feet on the cement wall, leaned back, and stared at the field. "Tell me what happened while I talked to Mr. Rayner. Obviously Nola's pitching a good game."

"Struck out five already." Nico turned his attention to the game. "But the Phillies' bats aren't exactly on fire."

"Yeah, but so long as Nola keeps the Cubbies off the bases, they don't need more than the two they have."

The inning ended and the next one began without either of them saying a word. Luke kept looking over his shoulder, but Kent never appeared.

God, even if Luke experienced the same electric spark between them, he so clearly wasn't over his ex.

Nico shivered, cold and tired. If he had been in the outside seat, he'd have probably excused himself to get a drink and set off home. Gone for a run, and finally, finally set up the air mattress that had arrived before they'd left.

Luke

Luke: Thought you were just getting drinks.

Kent: Seb isn't feeling well, so we left.

Luke: Sorry, hope he feels better.

Kent: Thanks, it's just a migraine, He'll be okay once he lies down.

Luke: What did you say to Nico?

Kent: You should ask him what he said. He cursed at me in Italian.

THAT SOUNDED LIKE NICO. Not the cursing part. But if he got mad at someone, he'd do it in Italian.

What happened that he swore at Kent? Whatever it was, it changed Nico's mood. His step lost its spring and his smiles had turned stiff.

Fuck, fuckety, fuck, fuck, fuck! This was supposed to be a time to relax and have fun, not ramp up his anxiety. Maybe bringing Nico had been a mistake. Not because of Nico, but he should have figured Kent would be jealous. Shit. *That* was part of the reason he asked Nico. Wasn't it?

The fact he couldn't answer it easily told Luke this had gotten more complicated. Almost from the time they met, Nico had been good to him. Things seemed to *just happen* at the time Luke needed something. There was always too much food for one person, so Luke should eat with him or it would go bad. When the summer was over, Nico planned to send the stuff he'd bought for the apartment to his family, so no reason for Luke to kick in half. There was never an expectation for anything in return.

But they were also just friends. Nico made that clear when he told Luke how his *next* boyfriend should treat him. Which was consistent with everything he'd said before. Nico wasn't ready to date.

So why had he agreed to practice with Luke?

Hell, why had Luke even suggested it?

Because he enjoyed the contact.

They both had.

And it didn't necessarily mean anything more than that. You didn't need to date someone to have sex. Friends with benefits, no strings attached, fuck buddies; those were things. They weren't really Luke's thing, but . . . .

No. They weren't. And he and Nico had to live together.

Complicating that would end badly.

And what was that bit about screening Luke's next boyfriends? One minute, Luke was sure Nico was about to suggest *they* try dating for real, and then Nico said that.

Okay, so the guy was hurting and didn't want to go there again soon. Luke got that. One hundred percent. He'd gone all in on Kent. Thought they were in love and were planning their future. Turned out, that reality existed only in Luke's heart and mind.

Trying to figure Nico out, however, was maddening.

He always did nice things for others, and then pretended it wasn't anything. Just like now. No way he really meant he'd okay Luke's next boyfriend.

The better question was, how did Luke get Nico to admit what he really wanted?

"Luke?" Hearing his name snapped him out of his thoughts. He turned at the same time as Nico. Mr. Rayner stood behind them, his ever-present smile as disarming as ever. "You have a minute?"

Rayner looked young to be a partner, but Luke had trouble guessing people's ages when they were between thirty-five and forty-five. He looked great for forty-five. His light brown hair, cut short, added to his youthful appearance. And he kept in shape.

Maybe he should suggest he go run with Nico. They'd push each other in a good way.

Focus! "Sure." He glanced at Nico, who looked as pale as he felt.

"Don't look so scared. I just want to introduce you and your friend to Ted Umstead, the managing partner." He nodded over his shoulder. "But we need to wait until between innings. Ted's a big fan and doesn't like being disturbed when the ball's in play."

He settled in the seat behind them. After a second, he leaned forward and extended his hand to Nico. "We didn't get a chance to speak when you arrived. Chris Rayner, call me Chris."

"Hi, Chris." Nico shook his hand. "Nico Amato."

The twinkle in Chris's eye threw Luke. "Can I assume someone related to you owns Amato's bakery in Brooklyn?"

Well, that's some shit. Did the entire world know about Amato's except Luke?

"My parents and grandparents own it."

"Small world. I grew up in Brightwaters on the Island. My grandparents took us kids to the bakery every year at Christmas."

That earned a smile from Nico. Talking about his family always improved his mood. "Then you'd have met Nonno, my grandfather. He loves to take care of the children."

"Yes, the owner used to come out whenever we showed up. Like he knew us personally."

"Yep, sounds like Nonno."

Chris shifted his attention to Luke. "Ted loves baseball. Played for Yale in his college days. Wanted to play pro ball, but he'd tore up his knee in the Ivy League tournament and never got drafted. Which is a lot of words to say he wants to meet you, and especially wants to talk baseball."

Was that why they hired him? Because he played baseball? His dad would have said who cares, whatever gets you in the door to prove you're worth hiring. "Should I ask if he played?"

"Can't hurt. He loves to talk about his playing days."

Luke tried to swallow his nerves, but it didn't work. "Okay."

"Since we have a minute, I want to tell you a few things I told him." Chris turned serious, and breathing suddenly became difficult. "And don't look so anxious, it's fine."

Nico rubbed Luke's his back comfortingly. Like a real boyfriend might. "It's all good, Luke. Breathe and relax."

The steady voice of reason to the rescue. He reached down and grabbed Nico's hand. Fake or not, he wanted to pretend right now it was real. That Nico was here for him. Meant every kind word, every soft touch. "Right. Breathe and relax. Got it."

"Nico's right, this *isn't* a big deal. I just wanted to tell you that I've talked you up a bit. Your work is good, and people like you. You probably don't remember, but I was on the call for your interview. We record them, and Ted no doubt listened to it before today. Don't be surprised if he brings up something you said during the interview."

Oh, crap. "I don't remember everything I said."

"Did you lie about anything?"

"No. Of course not."

Chris's laughter wasn't what he expected. "And that is why I knew I wanted you to work for me. You'd be surprised how much horse manure we get in an interview."

"Really?"

"You'd think people would realize we can sniff out lies pretty quickly these days, but it happens. And yes, we fact-checked you too." He winked. "Just be yourself. Ted's a really nice guy. He was my mentor when I interned . . . last century."

Nico's eyes darted behind Luke. "I think the inning's over. Ted and his wife are looking this way."

"That's our cue." Chris slapped his knees and pushed himself up. "C'mon, guys."

With his heart pounding, Luke released Nico's hand, turned to his left, and rose from his seat. Mr. and Mrs. Umstead had got up and awaited their arrival. Chris mirrored them on the upper level.

"I'm not sure if we should be offended that you sat as far from us as you could," Mr. Umstead said. His smile said he was joking, but Luke couldn't be sure.

"That's my fault, sir," Nico said. "When I first came out, I expected everyone would want to be out here to see the game. I tried to make it easier for everyone by sitting down here."

"Very considerate of you." He held out his hand to Luke. "Ted Umstead. Chris speaks very highly of you."

"Thank you, sir. I . . . Chris is really teaching me a lot."

"This is my wife, Janice."

"Pleased to meet you, Mrs. Umstead." Luke wasn't sure at first if he should shake her hand but held his out to be safe. She smiled as she accepted. "This is my boyfriend, Nico Amato."

They exchanged pleasantries until the time between innings ended. Chris did most of the talking, and Luke didn't remember much of what was said. Ted pointed out the eighth inning was about to start.

"I understand you play third base for Harrison's baseball team." Ted smiled at Luke.

"Yes, sir."

"It takes some grit to play the hot corner. I like that."

Luke wasn't sure Ted was speaking just about baseball. "It has its moments, but I love it."

"Since no one else is smart enough to realize these are the best seats, why don't you both join us?" Luke glanced at Chris, who gave him the barest of nods.

"Thank you, sir." He checked with Nico, who didn't object. "That's nice of you."

"No, thank you," he said. "It's always nice to sit with real fans."

THE BARTENDER BROUGHT everyone another drink. Luke sipped his. Sitting with the firm's managing partner, his supervising partner, and their spouses had its perks. It also brought with it a raft of dirty looks. People had to be invited to sit with Mr. Umstead, and invites were scarce. Good thing Nico had sat at the end of the row.

It also explained the dirty looks he'd gotten at the office. Chris was a favorite of Ted's and would probably join the executive suite soon. Taking Luke under his wing had been one thing. Getting invited to sit with the Umsteads suggested bigger things. At least to others. Luke didn't take an offer for granted.

"I'll have Luke give you my information," Nico said. "When your parents bring the kids, let me know. I'll probably be working during the holiday, but I'll make sure Nonno is too so he can greet them."

Ted wanted to talk baseball with Luke. As Chris said, he'd brought up his college playing days. While they talked, Chris and the "spouses" chatted. Clearly it had gotten around to Amato's Bakery.

"That's not really necessary. My kids always enjoy the trip."

"Not everything we do is necessary." Nico smiled, and his dimple showed. So damn cute. "Nonno is a great baker and loves dealing with the customers. He'll get a kick out of your visit. He's been much happier now that Mom and Dad take care of the business side of things."

"Which one are you?" Linda Rayner asked.

The Phillies' closer was entering the game, and Ted was listening to the spouses' conversation. Nico glanced at Luke, so he leaned closer. He was rewarded with a smile. A hand touched his, and Luke laced his fingers in Nico's. The gentle squeeze back told him everything was right in the world.

"I like to think I'm the two of them combined. I love talking to customers, I love to bake, and hopefully I'll be as good at the business as Papà. Plus, my cousin CJ wants to join the business, and my grandfather is thrilled."

"What about you? Is having your cousin as a partner a good thing?" Janice asked.

"The best. CJ's a natural."

"I always wanted to run my own business," Ted said. "But things work out as they do."

"Come visit the bakery over Christmas and it might dissuade you of the idea." Nico gave them a long-suffering look that had everyone laughing.

"Well said." Ted turned back to the field. "Let's see if Neris can lock this down for us."

THEY MADE it home later than Luke expected. When the game ended, Mr. Umstead went inside to socialize with his staff and asked Luke to join him. The attention rattled Luke's nerves, but Nico chatted with Mrs. Umstead and kept the mood light. After she laughed once too often, others seemed to crowd them.

Without missing a beat, the two continued their chat, trading funny stories that ensured people didn't discuss work. Chris and his wife had stayed, adding to the conversation in a way that suggested he and Mr. Umstead were close.

When they finally left, Mrs. Umstead—Janice, as she insisted they call her—made it a point to say how lovely it was to meet Luke and Nico and hoped they were *both* coming to the picnic in two weeks.

"Well, that was hardly fair," Nico said when they got home. "I didn't get to call in my favor before you extracted a new one from me."

"Excuse me?" Luke flopped down on the sofa in the living room. "I don't recall the words, 'Of course we'll be there, Janice,' coming from my mouth."

"What could I say at that point?" He plunked down next to Luke. "You clearly had a hand in them putting me on the spot."

Luke kicked off his shoes. "Right, it had nothing to do with you regaling everyone with stories of a certain nine-year-old covered in flour falling into a giant mixing vat and forcing their father and grandfather to hire someone to sanitize the equipment. Was that really true?"

Nico lounged back and exhaled. "I'm going to plead the Fifth."

"You do that a lot."

"Is it my fault you keep asking incriminating questions?" He winked before he got up. "I hope I wasn't too much."

"No. You were great." Luke grabbed Nico's hand and pulled himself up. "And, apparently, an international celebrity."

"Whatever. Kent seemed to think it was no big deal."

"Kent's opinion doesn't carry that much weight." Less with every interaction. "Did you really curse at him in Italian?"

"I'm going to guess I can't plead the Fifth on this." Nico walked into the kitchen. "Would you like some water?"

"Yes, please, to the water, and yes, you can invoke your right to remain silent, but it would be helpful to know the truth if it comes up."

"Remember when I told you the second-worst thing Nonna calls someone is a jackass?" When Luke nodded, Nico said, "I called him the worst thing Nonna calls people, *porca troia*."

Luke snorted. "The worst thing your grandmother calls people is pork triage?"

Nico laughed so hard he stopped reaching for the glasses. "No, *porca troia*. It's really quite vulgar. It means pig slut."

"Nonna actually *says* that?"

"Only when she really hates someone. She usually does this too." Nico put his hand between his teeth and shook it like he was biting into the finger.

"What does that mean?"

"Depends on who you ask, but to her it means if she sees you again, you'd better watch out."

"Wow, you never said Nonna was so scary." He noticed how easily he slipped into calling her Nonna and not "your nonna."

"Only when you make her mad." He filled a glass and handed it to Luke. "They heard everything."

Luke followed Nico's gaze. "Huh?"

"Ted and Janice. They heard me and Kent arguing. And I'm reasonably sure Janice, at least, understands Italian." Nico shrank from Luke. "I'm sorry if I embarrassed you in front of your work colleagues. Guess I'm no good at pretending to be someone's boyfriend either."

"Nico, you're . . ." He wasn't sure how to end that thought, so he reached for Nico's hand. Nico tried to pull away, but Luke didn't let that stop him. "You're amazing. You are. I wish . . . I wish you would see that."

He'd almost said something else, but that would've made things awkward between them. This was better.

"Fine, I'm amazing." Nico pulled back and leaned on the counter. "But I'm still sorry to be part of the office gossip for the next week. I wanted them to remember you because you're awesome, not because your boyfriend was involved in the most scandalous part of the day."

If he were honest, he didn't want to come to the attention of the managing partner because his ex decided to be a dickhead. "You can't be responsible for what Kent did. Plus, you stood up for me. That's what *I'll* remember."

"You deserve it." Nico's expression confused Luke. Almost sad, but not quite.

"Thank you. And since Mr. Umstead insisted we sit with them and *Janice* invited *us* to the picnic, they can't have cared what happened."

The tension drained from Nico. "True, and true."

"Thank you." Luke put the glass down and put his hands on Nico's shoulders. "For everything today."

This close, he wanted to kiss Nico, but he remembered their earlier conversation. The 'your next boyfriend' comment. Instead of a kiss, he settled for a hug. Those were safe between friends, right? Nico's arms slid around Luke, and he smiled.

"You're welcome." Nico didn't hold on for long. When he stepped back, he motioned toward the bedroom, not meeting Luke's eyes. "I'm gonna set up the air mattress."

The first day, Luke had been apprehensive about the sleeping situation. He barely knew Nico. It had taken an effort to fall asleep that night. Now, sleeping next to Nico felt comforting.

He walked into the bedroom as Nico opened the box.

"You know . . ." Luke waited until Nico looked up. There was something in Nico's expression that suggested this *was* an issue for him. "We could take turns using the air mattress if you want."

"And give up my first dibs on the bathroom? No chance. We have an agreement."

The glib answer fell flat in its delivery. Something had changed. As if Nico needed to get away.

"That's fine." He shrugged and turned around. "Just thought I'd offer."

"That's really nice of you, but it's fine. There's no reason for both of us to get used to a new mattress."

"Right." He should have figured Nico wouldn't put himself first.

CHAPTER ELEVEN

Nico

Isaiah: Seriously?

Nico: I so wouldn't lie. It's like it's not meant to be.

Isaiah: Maybe it isn't. But there are only 8 weeks left.

Nico: 6. I'm going home after the wedding.

Nico pulled the sheet back and climbed into bed. The king bed he still shared with Luke. "I'm sorry about this."

"What are you sorry for?" Luke rolled over and faced him, raising an amused brow. "Unless you created the leak?"

"As if. I should have paid for next-day shipping. The mattress wouldn't have gotten battered about and we'd have a working one by now."

"Geez, Nico. Eager to get away from me much?"

Yes. No.

Every night, I want to reach across the crisp sheets and touch you.

Ugh. "*Neither* of us wanted to share the bed this summer, right?"

"Yeah, but it hasn't been a problem," Luke said swiftly. "At least not for me."

Slam it home, Luke. The hug wasn't enough. "Yeah, me neither."

"Then this isn't a problem."

Nico shut his eyes. Even with his eyes closed, he *felt* Luke staring at him.

"And don't you dare order it again with next-day shipping," Luke said as if reading Nico's mind. "Given one fifth of the summer is gone, it makes even less sense to pay for it."

"Right."

"You're kinda quiet. You okay?" Luke asked softly.

Nico opened his eyes. Even in the semidarkness of the room, he could still make out Luke's perfect form under the sheets, those dark eyes. "I'm good. Why?"

"I dunno. Since your run-in with Kent, you seem out of sorts."

That was one way of putting it. "Nah, I'm over it."

"Don't let him get to you."

"Why did you ever date him?" Nico winced. The words spewed out before the logical side of his brain could throttle his emotions. "Sorry. That was wrong in about a bazillion ways."

"It's okay." The sheet moved as Luke rolled onto his back. "When he wants to be, he can be super nice. He's funny. We like a lot of the same things: sports, music, sci-fi/fantasy."

"You like sci-fi/fantasy?" How did Nico not know this?

"Totally. Our last date was to see *Avengers: Endgame*."

"Gotcha." Good thing he hadn't suggested they go see that when they were in New York.

"And he was really sweet when I was having family issues."

"I thought you and your family were tight?"

"We are, I meant . . . when I left last summer, Rosalie took it hard. She did the first two years as well, but this year seemed worse. Kent let me talk out my anxiety over what I thought I'd done to my sister. Which, before you say it, I know I didn't *do* anything, but I still felt responsible. He helped me deal with my irrational guilt.

"He had family issues, too. Different, but I guess we understood each other."

"That makes sense." Nico wanted to know more but wasn't sure how much he could ask. He rolled onto his side to face Luke. "How did you two meet?"

"At a frat party on campus." Luke repositioned on his side again and propped his head on his hand. Was it Nico's imagination, or was Luke a couple of inches closer to the middle? "He lives not far from Harrison. He had a friend who went to school there and came to the party. He goes to Penn State and was leaving a few days later."

"Ah, long-distance . . . or at least semi-long-distance."

"It wasn't too bad. I took the bus to see him on weekends, and he had a car. He came home a lot to help his parents."

"Is someone sick?"

"No." Luke moved his hand and punched up a pillow under his head. "They . . . Please don't repeat this. I mean, yes, he was an asshole to me, but I don't want his personal business all over the place."

"You don't have to tell me." *Yes, you really should.*

"I shouldn't, but it plays into why he said he broke up with me. His dad worked for a big company his whole career. Started there out of college and worked his way up. Kent's freshman year, his dad didn't get a promotion he'd been expecting. A year later, he got laid off."

"Wow, that's harsh." It probably explained a lot. Didn't excuse it, but certainly put it in context.

"No and yes. It's like the military. There are fewer spots the higher you go up. I mean, there is only one CEO, right? If you get passed over a couple of times, it generally means you're not one of their top people and you're not going to move up. In the military, if you don't get promoted beyond a certain rank, they make you retire."

"I guess that makes sense. Can't be easy to manage a bunch of bitter people who feel they should be the boss not you."

"That's it. But I don't think his dad expected it was his time. Anyway, it was a problem for the family. Kent's grandparents funded his college fund, so that wasn't a problem, but . . . his parents didn't plan for his dad to be laid off at fifty-three."

"Who does?"

"Right, but according to Kent, they planned to catch up on their savings after Kent finished school."

"Wow. That's rough. No savings and no way to catch up." Nico only half understood. His family were savers. Probably because the bakery didn't earn the same each month or year.

"It got worse. His dad started drinking, which didn't help him find a job. And he regretted picking the safety of a corporate job over doing other things."

"I get that." But as he told Kent, that didn't give him the right to be an asshat to Luke.

"Well, my 'boring goals' are going to leave me in the same boat one day."

The fucker actually told Luke that? Talk about assholery. "There are so many things wrong with that."

"Maybe, but it's true. I want a steady job. I like to be organized, have a routine. I'm, ah, kinda boring."

"No, you're smart. Having a plan to get what you want isn't stupid. Thinking you can skip doing the hard work today and catch up later is stupid. And that's what his father did. It might even be why he got laid off in the first place."

"That's not fair."

"Yes, it is." Nico sat up as if that would make his arguments more compelling. "My parents always save first. If they couldn't afford a vacation or a new car without sacrificing their savings, they did without or found other ways. They didn't spend now and plan to catch up later.

"It's the same with the bakery. They don't skip maintenance when it needs to be done to do it sometime in the future. I don't know what happened to his dad's job, but he had the power to control the other part and didn't. Do *not* second-guess your plans because of something Kent said. Because, sooner or later, he will realize you are right and he is wrong."

Luke sat up and crushed Nico into a warm, skin-filled hug that shattered shivers through him. "Thanks, Nico. I mean, I know you're right, but hearing it from someone else really helps."

Nico let himself hold on tightly for a few more seconds and then flopped back onto his soft pillow. "And one more thing. Boring? Fuck that. You're fun."

WARMTH SOAKED AROUND NICO. Cozier than the blankets usually were. He snuggled into it—

Nico blinked through the haze of sleep, not sure he wasn't dreaming. The heat blazing against his back and stomach shifted, intensified. Nico caught his breath, heartrate ramping up. He felt each individual finger splayed against his stomach sizzling shivers into him.

Luke was wrapped around him.

Luke had crossed the Rubicon and invaded Rome.

And judging how far into the middle of the mattress Nico had rolled, Rome had welcomed the incursion.

Nico shut his eyes. *Just one more moment absorbing how good this feels.* One moment imagining this was real.

Hot breath trickled over his nape, and Luke murmured, sleepily rutting his hard length against Nico's ass cheek.

Nico's dick jumped and he gritted his teeth against the aching arousal swamping his body. *Moment over.*

"Luke?" He squeezed the hand on his abs, gently prying Luke's fingers from him. "I need to get up."

"Huh?" Nico waited for the sleepy haze to pass. *Three, two—* "What? Oh, crap!"

Luke snatched his arm back and pulled away. Nico rolled over, barely suppressing a grin.

"Shit! I'm sorry. Did I . . .?" Luke gestured pointedly. Intimately.

"You were a perfect gentleman." He waggled his eyebrows. "As much of a gentleman as you can be while holding someone."

"Oh, man. I'm so sorry. I don't remember how it happened." He closed his eyes and flexed his fingers.

"Chill. It's fine. I mean, unless you're upset you touched me?"

"What? No! I mean, I'm sorry I did that without your permission, but I'm not sorry, I mean, yes, I am, but not because I was . . . Ugh!" He took a deep breath and said, "I'm not weirded out touching you. I just feel like I crossed a line."

"If I said it felt nice waking up that way, would that make it better or worse?"

"Was it?"

Nico laughed. "No way. You can't answer me with a question."

"Fine, if you're not mad, then I feel better."

"Then feel better." He tossed the sheet back. "I'm not mad. Well, other than at myself for agreeing to work Sunday at eight."

"Oh, right. First day on the job. I thought you weren't going to work weekends?"

"I'm not supposed to, but someone has a sick kid and they asked if I'd fill in." He stretched for a second before he remembered he was rock-hard and showing. As he turned toward the dresser, he didn't miss Luke watching.

So much for defusing the situation.

"They must trust you if your first day is a weekend."

"That, or they're desperate." Nico flicked on the bathroom light. "I'll leave the door unlocked."

Luke gaped at him, and Nico winked. "For you to use the bathroom," he clarified. "Since you're, you know, *up*."

Luke glanced down; the thin sheet hid nothing. He shifted, giving a good-humored laugh that didn't make Nico like him more. Nope, not one bit . . .

He escaped into the bathroom and hit the shower. Water sluiced over his taut skin, and Nico sagged back against the wall.

Not one itty bit.

Fuuuuuck.

Elisa: Elliott's family invited everyone to dinner in Philly next weekend.

Nico: I hope no one thinks they're staying with me.

Elisa: Doofus. No, but can you help find a hotel for them?

Nico: Elliott did this. Have him find the hotel. He knows the city better than I do.

"THANK YOU. COME SEE US AGAIN." Nico handed the bag to the customer and moved away from the register.

It had taken five minutes to figure out what Esposito's had for sale and where to find things. Vito, an employee who must have been with them since Guido Esposito opened the shop a hundred years ago, ran the register.

Business had been steady, heavy even, leaving no time to consider what to do about Luke. He tried to sort it out on the walk to the market, but that left him more confused than settled. The mild flirting, the little touches, making out when buzzed, those pointed toward Luke liking Nico. Countering that was Kent.

In Nico's book, the guy sucked big time. Pig slut was too nice an insult. Luke, however, still saw the good times. The moments when Kent had come through for him, even when he had his own problems. He knew from experience those things were hard for the heart to forget.

And Luke hadn't. Not even close.

Outwardly, Luke showed anger toward his ex, but as soon as a text from Kent arrived, he rushed to answer. Nico couldn't compete with that. No one could.

And even if Nico could . . . would Luke still like the other him? The colorful him who loved the flair for the dramatic. Who missed his designer clothes—blazers, scarfs, and shoes—God, his *shoes*.

He'd trusted that Tomas liked him. The first guy in forever he actually thought dug him for *him*, and look how that had turned out.

Why should he expect things to turn out differently with Luke?

Nico pinched his nose. He should stop this wildly-out-of-control crush on Luke. He was afraid the next nice thing Luke did, the next kind thing he said, Nico would do something stupid.

"Hey, kid."

Nico plastered on his fake smile and turned toward the older man. "Whatcha need, Vito?"

"Nothing, kid." He smiled like he was Zio Vito. "I just wanted to say I'm impressed. You're pretty good at selling."

"I've worked at my family's bakery since I was twelve. Nonno was an amazing teacher."

"Your family owns a bakery? Which one? Does Rocco know?"

Nico admired the loyalty. "Rocco knows. That's why he hired me. I already know the goods."

Vito rubbed his chin as if he couldn't wrap his head around what he'd heard. "You do know what we're selling."

Better than Vito, if he had to guess. Nico could make anything in the display case. Had made everything at one time or another. "Thanks. Nonno and Papà taught me everything they know."

"What bakery?"

"Amato's in New York."

"Never heard of 'em. Are you guys any good?"

He wanted to say they were the third-biggest Italian bakery in the country, but it probably wouldn't go over well. Vito was loyal, and Nico might have to work with him again. "Not bad. But not as good as Esposito's."

Vito gave him the horns. "You're a smooth talker. And you're doing so well, you don't need me up there. Let's me rest my legs."

A customer walked up, saving Nico from responding. He was fine with handling all the customers, even if he was earning half of Vito's paycheck for him. It gave him an outlet to avoid thinking about Luke.

Reality, however, was going to come crashing back in about fifteen minutes when his shift ended.

He flicked open the bag, put two sweet rolls inside, and decided he'd deal with Luke when it was time. Not a minute before.

Luke

Coury: You did what?

Luke: It's complicated.

Coury: That's one word for it.

Luke: You're not helping.

LUKE HAD HELD Nico last night. Maybe most of the night.

He didn't remember how it happened, hadn't *meant* for it to happen. But. There had been that dream. That very sexy dream. Where Nico had rolled atop him, had kissed him hard, had whispered in Luke's ear as he'd groped Luke's dick and—

Luke scrubbed his flushed face.

Nico was kind to call him a gentleman, because the things they did in that dream were far from gentlemanly.

Luke picked up his phone for the . . . he lost track of how many times it had been—checking for a message. Still nothing.

Nico said he was only working four hours. His shift should have ended three hours ago, so where was he? Damn, Luke hated not being able to read Nico better.

"Stop." He exhaled slowly.

They were roommates and friends, not boyfriends. Nico didn't need to check in with him. Moreover, Nico wouldn't think Luke expected that. Because he shouldn't. They. Were. Friends.

Luke glanced at the table, set for two. So much for surprising Nico with lunch. Probably too much anyway.

Whatever he didn't eat, he could take for lunch tomorrow.

Mrs. R had recommended the deli two blocks over. They had the best Italian hoagie with the works in walking distance. Evidently if one wanted to drive, better could be had, but these were plenty good enough. She didn't seem the type to do much walking, so he bought an extra one and dropped it off on his way upstairs.

Just like Nico would have done.

The door opened behind him, and he swiveled around.

Nico entered the room, gaze sweeping from him to the table. He halted abruptly.

Luke's palms sweated.

"Oh. Are you expecting company?" Nico shifted the bag in his left hand, his shoulders seemingly deflating. "Give me a few minutes to change and I'll, ah, get out of your way."

"What? No, wait!" Luke quick-stepped across the room.

Nico froze as his eyes darted from the table to Luke, and he shrank back from him. "Yes?"

"I thought I'd surprise you with lunch after your first day at the bakery. Kinda like you made me dinner after my first day of work."

A cautious frown broke over Nico's expression, growing deeper as he looked from Luke to the table and back again.

Luke shifted, jamming his hands into his pockets. "You already ate, right?"

"Actually, no," Nico said slowly. "I ended up staying later because the person who was supposed to replace me didn't show." He held up the bag. "A thank-you gift from Rocco."

"I hope he also paid you money for the extra hours."

That comment kicked Nico out of whatever wary thoughts he'd been having. "Of course. I don't work for cannolis. Even as kids, Nonno paid us when we helped at the shop."

"That's good. That you got paid."

Luke stumbled for what to say. Clearly Nico seemed apprehensive about the lunch.

Was Nico worrying Luke was coming on to him?

Of course he was.

How could he not after the way they'd woken this morning?

"It's just lunch," Luke said, when Nico stared at the table again.

Nico snapped toward him. "Right. Sure. Just lunch. That you waited until"—he tapped the screen of his watch—"three thirty-five for me to eat?"

Luke cursed himself for foisting an uncomfortable situation on Nico. He tried shrugging it off. "Like you say, it's no fun to eat alone."

It's no fun to eat alone?

That's what Luke went with?

He was an idiot.

He bowed his head as Nico put the bag in the kitchen. Then

Nico brushed past, hesitated, and whispered a kiss over Luke's cheek. "Let me clean up, and I'll be right back."

Nico beelined to their bedroom, and Luke's hand drifted to his cheek.

What did that mean?

LUKE AND NICO played a game of gaze-tag over lunch. Taking turns catching the other looking and hurriedly refocusing on their hoagies.

Luke didn't bring up the kiss to his cheek, or last night, but the weight of it grew with every bite.

When they finished their sandwiches, they looked longingly at their empty plates.

"That was so good," Nico said energetically. As if to break the tension. "Great call by Mrs. R."

"I was worried it wouldn't live up to your New York standards."

Nico finished his water and reached for the pitcher. "Truth? Delis don't make their own prosciutto, capicola, salami, or provolone. They all buy from the same places. So long as they use quality meats and good bread—and this place does—they're all going to taste about the same."

Luke smiled at the slight hesitation in Nico's voice when he pronounced "prosciutto." "Yeah, but since New York delis used gabagool and brahjzoot, I was worried these would be disappointing."

Glass to his lips, Nico spit-laughed. Water came out his nose, and he coughed so hard he put a hand on the table to brace himself.

"Look up." Luke pointed to the ceiling, smiling. "I have it on good authority that works."

Nico tilted his head back and slowly gained control. When he stopped coughing, he looked into his glass and frowned. "Well, I'm not drinking that."

"Sorry."

"Don't be, that was hilarious." Nico grabbed a clean glass and snatched the dish towel from the rack. "Next time warn me when you're going to toss my idiosyncrasies back at me."

"That would ruin the effect."

"Brat." Nico refilled both their glasses and took his seat. "Let's have dessert."

Nico pulled two cannolis from the white wax-treated bag and put one each on two plates. "These are a rare treat."

"What? Did Rocco make 'em with special filling?"

"Eww." Nico's face squished up like he'd eaten something foul. "Do not ever go there again."

Luke laughed. "Why are they so rare?"

"They were free."

"Why is *that* so rare? Do they always make you pay for them?"

"Almost always, yes. I mean, if you worked for Macy's, would they give you a shirt if you asked?"

Luke snorted. "Clearly you had that canned answer ready. Had this discussion before?"

"Many times. New employees almost always ask for a free pastry, especially at the end of the day if we have a lot left over." Nico's tongue darted out over the tip of his thumb and he licked off a splotch of cream.

The image went straight to Luke's groin. He shifted in his seat. "That makes total sense."

"This might not be the best time to ask this, since I'm plying you with utter perfection, but Elliott asked my parents and grandparents to come to dinner in Philly next weekend. His family lives in the suburbs." Nico snuck a peek over his cannoli and averted his eyes quickly. "He invited us too."

"Us? I thought your sister knew there isn't a real us?" Yet. Ever?

"She does, and so does Elliott, I think." He set his cannoli down. "My parents asked if you were invited and Elisa didn't know how to answer that, so she said yes."

"Oh." So Nico was calling in his favor? "Next weekend?"

"Yeah." Squaring his shoulders, Nico looked Luke in the eye. "But no pressure. Really. If it feels weird, say no. My family won't think it's weird if you're not there."

If he didn't *need* to bring a date, why was Nico asking? "So you're not calling in your favor?"

"No, this isn't a 'favor', it's just a favor." Nico shrugged, and they both laughed. "I love my family, but I could use a friend to hang with. If you can make it, I'd appreciate it, if not, it's all good."

"Yeah?" Luke tapped his fork to his water glass and smirked. "Will there be more practicing?"

"Definitely." He wiggled his eyebrows. "Gotta train Elliott's family before the reception."

Luke's phone buzzed, and on instinct he pulled it out.

Kent: Do you know where the picnic is and what time it starts?

No way Kent didn't know this. Hell, Luke knew off the top of his head. What was Kent up to?

Luke: No.

"Kent?" Nico asked.

"Yeah, he's being a butthead." He went to put the phone away, but it vibrated again.

Kent: C'mon. I know you know. We're on the boat and Seb needs to check his calendar.

That was supposed to make him *more* inclined to help?

Luke: I'm busy. Check your emails.

After angrily typing his reply, Luke pushed the phone into his pocket. Nico watched him with an oddly somber expression. "Sorry."

"No worries. Exes are hard." That fake smile returned. "That's why I'm taking a break from dating."

"Right." That clarified things. The kiss on the cheek was nothing, then. Just a thank you for lunch. "About next weekend, I don't . . ."

Nico's expression fell, and the sight jolted through Luke. "It's cool. I'll tell my family—"

"I don't want to miss it."

"You don't?" Nico perked up. "You want to go?"

He gave Nico a tiny smirk. "If that's what you want."

"Yeah, of course! I wasn't sure you'd want to. I mean . . ."

"I like your family. It'll be fun." *Even if it rubs what I want in front of my face.* "Wanna go for a run later?"

"Sure. After we have time to digest."

Food wasn't the only thing Luke needed to digest.

CHAPTER TWELVE

Nico

Nico: The Forsythe? Are you kidding me?

Elisa: What's wrong with the Forsythe? It's a nice hotel.

Nico: Luke's ex is dating a Forsythe.

Elisa: So? They're staying there overnight, we're not eating there.

Elisa was right. It didn't matter. Luke wouldn't care. He never said anything bad about Sebastian.

So why did Nico feel like this was a betrayal?

Because he had it bad for Luke and wanted to protect him.

Nico felt Luke climb into his side of the bed, and Nico dropped his phone on the nightstand and curled into the blankets. His heart hammered, and he told himself to calm down. Just because they ended up wrapped like pretzels once, didn't mean it'd happen again.

Luke shifted and stilled, and Nico relaxed, disappointment flaring through him.

What had he hoped? After one tiny kiss on Luke's cheek, he'd brazenly wrap him into a hug and whisper how much he liked him? How much he wanted to give this a go? How much he liked Nico for Nico?

WARM, wriggly movement woke Nico from a deep sleep. He hummed, and hair tickled his nose. *Hair*?

He jolted awake.

Nico was curled around Luke, one arm draped over his tight, flat stomach. And Luke was snuggling back into him.

Holy *shit*. It was happening again. But this time he was hugging Luke with a raging hard-on. Something Luke had to notice grinding against his supple ass.

"Luke?" Nico's voice came out low and husky. "What are we doing?"

"You reached for me," Luke whispered back, voice startlingly awake. "I'm just going with it."

Luke wrapped his arm around Nico's as if to prevent him from pulling away, and Nico's heart hitched. Holding Luke felt like a dream.

Nico's fingers absently traced the outline of Luke's left nipple. Luke moaned softly, pressing back hard against his front, soaking Nico with his heat.

Nico pushed into it, grinding his straining cock into Luke muscular ass. The friction amped Nico's lust for his roommate to a new high.

Lust.

That was all this was between them. They were just horny and needed release.

Luke rolled around and faced Nico, noses bumping. "I think you said we needed more practice before dinner tomorrow."

"Didn't get enough practice in New York?"

Even in the darkness of the room, Luke's eyes twinkled mischievously. "I have a different kind of practice in mind for tonight."

And there was the excuse. Just practice. Just fooling around. Just for tonight.

Nico hesitated. This wasn't a good idea, with the crush he had on the guy. They shouldn't . . .

Unless. Maybe they could fuck away this electric connection between them? Maybe then Nico could move on from liking Luke so hard.

Nico curved a hand around Luke's hip to his firm ass. "I think you just want to get off with someone."

"Not just someone." His thumb ran along Nico's lower lip.

Nico's pulse doubled. "What?"

"Nothing." Luke cupped Nico's face. "Kiss me."

Nico abandoned rational thought and crushed his lips against Luke's.

A hot, eager tongue pushed into his mouth, and Nico hauled Luke closer. Their legs tangled, their hard dicks rubbed, their stomachs undulated. Luke gripped him tight, tight, tight, and Nico scrabbled to get tighter still. Sensation fired through his nerve endings, and Nico met every slick thrust of Luke's tongue.

Luke gasped between gulps of air, and Nico panted like he'd run ten miles.

Their gazes connected in the dark, amazement glittering between them.

Easily the hottest kiss of Nico's life.

Nico caressed Luke's cheek, thumb rubbing gentle circles over his skin. "We should keep practicing."

Luke tugged Nico, and Nico rolled on top of him. He pushed

his torso up enough to admire the way Luke thrust his chin up, neck straining as their cocks ground together. Every slide of his cock over Luke's spiraled his lust, his need for more connection.

Luke's hands skated under Nico's boxers, not breaking their kiss. Nico flexed his glutes, and Luke squeezed them with perfect pressure. His underwear slid over his ass, and Nico raised his hips. His cock sprang free as Luke shoved the fabric to Nico's thighs.

"This needs to go too," Luke murmured, grabbing the hem of Nico's shirt and peeling it over his head.

"No fair." Nico kicked off his boxers. "You still have all your clothes on."

"Whatcha gonna do about that?" Luke waggled his eyebrows.

Nico bent down as if to kiss Luke and shifted at the last second. He grabbed Luke's cotton trunks and freed his leaking cock.

He winked, dipped his head, and swallowed most of Luke's considerable length.

Luke slapped the mattress and clutched at the sheets. "Fuck!"

Nico's cock jumped at the debauched groan. He sealed his lips around Luke and rubbed the flat of his tongue over him. Luke squirmed, his breath hitching with indecipherable words. Curses, maybe. Nico loved how Luke watched him with dark eyes, how he trembled and bucked under Nico's ministrations. Loved how Luke let go and gave in to his pleasure.

Nico grabbed the base of Luke's cock and pulled back until his lips slid off the head with a loud pop.

Luke flopped back hard onto his pillow. "Christ, Nico!"

"Like that, do you?" Nico locked his eyes on Luke's as he swiped his tongue over the glans again. "Or should I stop?"

"Don't you dare."

Nico grinned and wrapped his lips around Luke's dick.

Luke was a bit too long for Nico to take him all in, at least from this position, but he managed to get far enough down that

Luke's pubes tickled his nose. Breathing deep, he took in the hot-as-fuck guy writhing under him. Like everything else about him, Luke's scent drove Nico crazy. He could spend hours enjoying Luke's body.

He drew up until his teeth gently grazed the tip of Luke's head, and then plunged down, tongue firmly on the underside of the shaft.

"Nico!" The urgency in Luke's voice had Nico wrapping a hand around his base for extra friction. "If you don't . . . ah, fuck!"

Luke thrust up as Nico pushed down and Luke frantically fucked his throat. His arms and legs flailed, and Nico squeezed one mound of his ass, pushing Luke deeper into him.

"Fuck, I'm gonna come. I'm gonna . . . nhhh."

The first shot sprayed inside Nico's mouth. He kept his mouth locked just below the head and used his fingers to extract the rest of his prize for a blowjob well done.

When Luke stopped convulsing, Nico drew back slow, eliciting a hiss of breath. He sucked the last bit of come off his fingers before raking his eyes up Luke's body until their eyes met.

"That. Was. Incredible," Luke said, with a satisfied smile. "You totally *don't* need the practice."

Nico crawled up Luke's body until their lips were inches apart. "You can never get too much practice doing that."

Luke

LUKE CUPPED the back of Nico's head and pulled him in for a deep kiss. He tasted his own come, and that just made the kiss hotter. Holy hell, watching Nico go down on him like that . . . watching him lick his fingers—

Nico groaned into the kiss, and Luke flipped him over.

"I think I should get some practice, too." He covered Nico's mouth again, his still hard cock brushing over Nico's.

Christ, he never stayed hard this long. He was so horny, it was like he hadn't just exploded in one of the best orgasms of his life. *The things you do to me, Nico.*

Their lips parted, and they both hauled in lungfuls of air. Nico's arousal-damp skin clamped against Luke's, and Luke slithered down his amazing body.

He kissed the head of Nico's leaking cock.

Nico had given him the best blowjob of his life, and while Luke might not be able to match him, he intended to try.

Luke swiped a tongue over the underside of Nico's cock, and Nico shivered.

Emboldened, Luke licked around Nico's head, greedily lapping the precome. He slid a finger under the shaft and swallowed as much as his mouth would allow. He mimicked Nico's technique, using his tongue to increase the sensation. A deep moan rewarded his efforts.

"God, that's good! Oh yeah, keep doing that," Nico said on a breathy moan.

Nico clutched the sheets. His body tensed and thrust up. Luke used his free hand to hold Nico down, but as Luke moved faster, Nico thrashed under him like he'd been hit with electricity.

"Can't . . . gonna . . . Luuuuuuke!"

Nico shot into Luke's hungry mouth, then fired off several quick bursts. Luke didn't release his cock until Nico's body unclenched and he relaxed back onto the mattress. With a slow sucking motion, he gradually raised his head until only the tip touched his lips. After a gentle kiss, Luke swallowed and looked up.

Nico's eyes were closed, and his chest rose and fell in rapid succession.

Luke blanketed Nico's body with his and rested his head next to Nico's ear.

"Definitely can't get too much practice doing that."

Arms wrapped around his back, and Luke relaxed onto Nico's tight body. Enjoying the after-sex contact, he closed his eyes.

Coury: You had sex with Nico?!?

Luke: Don't make it sound incestuous! It just happened.

Coury: Sex doesn't, 'just happen.' Are things really weird now?

Luke: Not sure, Nico got up early.

Coury: Things are weird.

LUKE DROPPED his phone on the bed and sighed. Were they? Maybe, or maybe they were good. Nico had said he had a lot to do today.

"Hi, Rocco." Nico's voice trailed from the other room.

At least Nico hadn't run out of the apartment. And what was that smell? Coffee! Luke stretched and tossed back the sheet.

"Sorry, I can't today."

Nico had thrown his shirt and shorts somewhere. God, that had been hot. Remembering his clothes coming off sent a rush of blood to his cock.

"I'm sorry Vito is sick, but my family is coming soon, and I need to get ready for them."

Focus. Luke needed to speak to Nico before he ran off for the day. His shirt was by his side of the bed and his shorts were . . . in the corner near the bathroom? Nico must've been in a hurry to get rid of them.

Luke snagged his boxers on the way to pee.

"No, I can't work tomorrow either. Sorry."

Good for Nico. They were taking advantage of him, asking him to work for a pittance so they could stay home. He flushed the toilet and swished some mouthwash for a second.

". . . like a plan. I'll see you Monday." Something hit the counter hard. Luke hoped Nico hadn't broken his phone. "Ugh!"

Nico was pouring coffee when Luke left the bedroom. He looked up and smiled. A real one. "Hey. Sorry if I woke you."

"You didn't," Luke assured him, and Nico handed him a cup. "Thanks."

"I got up to use the bathroom and saw a missed call from Esposito's." He took a sip and leaned back on the counter. "I tried to be quiet, but I guess not."

"Nah, you were good. I was up when you called." Luke's cup of java called to him. Another of Nico's good qualities: he made excellent coffee. "Let me guess, they wanted you to come in today."

"Heard that, did you?" He glanced down at his feet. "I'm not sure if I should be angry or flattered. Unfortunately, that's one of the downsides of running a small business: when someone calls out, the owner has to cover."

"Are you speaking from experience?"

"No and yes. We're much bigger than Esposito's. There are usually enough people working that if someone calls out, they can generally get by. But sometimes my parents had to go in." He rolled his eyes. "Or they sent me."

They laughed for a moment, and an uneasy silence followed. Luke took another sip and let his cup linger. How to approach the elephant in the room? "So, last night . . ."

Nico smiled wildly and shrugged. "Yeah. I had fun."

Fun. Something about the blasé way Nico said it had Luke's gut falling to his feet. "Um, me too. So we're okay?"

"Why wouldn't we be?" Nico's smile vanished. "Are *you* okay?"

"I'm great. It's just, I don't want it to come between us. You know, now that we crossed that line."

Nico looked at the wall. "Nothing has changed. It was just some fun, right?"

That word again. "Right. Fun."

"If this weirds you out, I can sleep on the couch until the mattress gets here." Nico continued avoiding Luke's gaze.

"I'm not weirded out if you're not."

"Nope, I'm good too."

If he was good, why not look at him? "What time do we head out to dinner with your family?"

"Mom said she'll call when they leave." He finished his coffee. "Knowing my parents, they'll probably swing by here first. Too curious for their own good."

"Oh, okay. Cool." He moved closer and rubbed Nico's arm. "Thanks for making the coffee. I'll miss this when we go back to school."

"I'll come by every morning at seven with your coffee."

Nico might be joking, but the thought of *not* seeing him every morning bothered Luke. "Or I could come to your room. That way it won't get cold."

"That's so practical."

Practical. That was Luke, all right. He shrugged it off. "I guess we should clean this place up for your parents. What's first on our list?"

"Our list?" Nico shook his head. "Coming to dinner is all you need to do. I'll take care of cleaning."

"Fuhgeddaboudit. I live here too. I'll help."

"Fuhgeddaboudit? Really?"

What? "Did I use it wrong?"

"Nope. It was perfect. I just never heard you say that before."

"I pick up a few things here and there." *Like how wildly you kiss when I squeeze your ass.* Okay, bad idea to go there. Luke nodded toward their room. “We should shower before we clean the bathroom.”

“Together?” Nico wiggled his eyebrows.

Oh, God. How hot would that be? “Seriously?”

“Sadly, no. We’d never get any work done.” He pouted. “Rain check?”

“Sure,” Luke said with a wink, “but don’t think I won’t use it.”

CHAPTER THIRTEEN

Luke

Nico's family didn't like Elliott's parents.

Especially Nonno, who scowled and muttered at his food.

Elliott's father had clearly researched Amato's bakery. His prying questions about sales and profits were met with polite deflections until Elisa elbowed Elliott, and Elliott asked his father to stop talking business.

The conversation turned to their boat, vacation house, trips, and stock portfolio.

Luke felt uncomfortable on the Amatos behalf and embarrassed for Elliott and Elisa.

He stirred in his chair, foot knocking into Nico's next to him. He stopped himself from murmuring an apology. Why say sorry when you weren't?

In fact, why move it back at all?

Nico's gaze shot to his, brown eyes glittering with a smile.

Luke rubbed Nico's foot, and Nico tentatively pressed back. He took a sip of wine and missed his mouth, spilling a drop onto his purple sports jacket. Again, Nico had dressed up for the occasion, and again Luke couldn't help noticing how much more comfortable Nico seemed. Like the clothes or the color boosted his confidence. It was almost too much—the confidence, that was. Nico was sexy enough as it was—

Luke swallowed hard, staring at Nico dabbing his jacket with a napkin.

Nonna muttered into his ear, and Nico rolled his eyes.

"What did Nonna say to you?" Luke asked, smoothing a kink in Nico's lapel.

Nico leaned toward him, keeping his voice low. His breath hit Luke over the bridge of his nose, eliciting a shiver. "She said they were uncouth. You don't talk about money at dinner. Especially with people you just met."

"Your poor dad. He's taken the brunt of it."

"He's also the most patient."

"So, Nico," Mrs. Randall said loudly, catching everyone's attention. "I've never seen such a shiny purple sports coat before. Certainly not here in *our* club."

Nico stiffened, his gaze darted to Luke, and his checks flushed. Nonna hissed in Italian.

"Excuse me?" Mrs. Randall said indignantly.

Luke narrowed his eyes on the woman. How dare she speak to Nico like that? "She said no one who comes *here* looks half as good as Nico does." Luke slid his fingers over the back of Nico's and interlocked them. "Nico looks amazing."

All eyes swiveled to him and Nico. Luke didn't care what they thought of his outburst. No way he'd sit there and let Nico take that shit. Nico rocked his outfit. So damn handsome.

Elisa beamed at him, and Nico squeezed his fingers around Luke's and squared his shoulders.

"A bit of color helps to brighten people's day." He gave Mrs. Randall his fake smile. "I promise to wear a staid and boring black tux to the wedding."

"Only because you couldn't find one in purple, boo." Elisa's joke elicited a nervous laugh from Elliott. "But I'm sure you can find a cummerbund that gives you a hint of color."

The mood didn't improve much. Elisa and Elliott tried their best to keep things light, but it was a wasted effort. Nico refilled his wineglass every time it got low. When he reached for the bottle again, Luke grabbed his hand. "Let's go for a walk?"

Nico's defiant glare was dispelled by Nonna patting his arm. She whispered to her grandson, and Nico's face lit with a smile. He kissed her cheek and pushed his chair back. "If you'll excuse us for a bit. We're going to get some air."

As soon as they reached the aisle, Luke reached for Nico's hand. He felt a gentle squeeze as their fingers laced together.

Several people in the club stared at them. Most smiled, but not all. One woman hissed disgust. And another man made a puking gesture.

Luke barely refrained from flipping him off, and he yanked Nico back when he shifted in the man's direction.

He spotted a tall table with two stools in the bar area and headed to them. Nico shimmied onto the seat across from Luke.

"Oh my, it's *so* much fresher in here." Nico took an exaggerated breath, throwing his arms out in the process. "You can practically smell farmland."

Luke bit back a smile. "That's so original. I've never heard that before."

Nico's face lit up in horror, and he settled his hand on top of Luke's. "You worked on a farm. I didn't mean to insult you. I was just, you know . . ." His left hand swooshed around.

"Just being Nico?" He used his free hand to rub Nico's. The contact scattered goose bumps up his arm. "Good thing I like you."

Nico swept the compliment aside, frowning. Like maybe he didn't trust it. "If we're not here for dairy air, why did you want to leave?"

"You looked like you needed a break."

"Because I was drinking so much?" A note of defiance shaded Nico's voice.

"It's not that you're drinking, it's *why* you're drinking. Every time Mrs. Randall said something, you reached for your wine."

"I feel sorry for Elisa. She's got to deal with them." Nico grimaced. "Didn't you wonder why my parents never met them? I mean, they've been dating two years and are getting married in a month."

"This is the first time they've met? I thought only your grandparents hadn't met them."

"Nope. My parents hadn't either." Nico looked toward the main restaurant. "Elliott is a bit impressed by money, but even he recognizes they're . . . they're . . ."

"Uncouth?" Luke tilted his head and smiled.

"Right, let's go with that."

Luke snickered. "That isn't what Nonna said, is it?"

"*Omertà*." Nico put his fingers by his lips and pretended to turn a lock.

"O mare ta?"

"*Omertà*. You don't snitch on your family. It's Sicilian and generally refers to the mafia. You don't talk to the cops, and the family takes care of your family if you go to jail." He looked Luke in the eye, cocking his head to one side as if trying to figure something out. "Thank you for standing up for me. Um, before."

"I meant every word. You look fantastic."

Nico dragged his gaze away and bit his lip. He pinched the jacket fabric. "I might have worn it to test something."

"Test what?"

Nico's Adam's apple jutted.

A waitress came by, interrupting them. Luke sighed and ordered two glasses of white wine. Nico arched a brow and mouthed "Two?"

"One for you. Like I said, it wasn't that you were drinking, it was why you were drinking. Now, what were you trying to test?"

Nico waved it off. "I just wore it to get a reaction." He paused. "Mrs. Randall certainly pulled through."

"So what *did* Nonna say when Mrs. Randall dissed your jacket? I'm sure it wasn't how handsome you look."

"Ahh, so the wine is to get me drunk so I'll violate the code of silence?"

"Will it work?"

Nico laughed. "Basically she said if someone didn't put that woman in her place, she'd do it herself." Nico blushed. "And then you swept in."

"I like this knight-in-shining-armor story you're telling."

Nico snorted just as the waitress returned with their drinks.

Luke told her to put it on the Randall's tab.

Nico snickered softly after she left. "They'll probably fuss about that."

"So? They invited us to dinner at *their* club." Luke raised his glass. "Besides, did you hear them talk about how much money they have?"

"Who didn't?"

Luke sipped. "Now get back to that story you were telling. With the handsome knight saving the evening."

"Handsome?" Nico squished his nose. "Hmm."

Luke playfully kicked Nico's foot, and Nico threw his head back in a laugh. "All right, all right. He was pretty damn handsome."

Nico

NICO WAS BUZZED, and not just from the wine.

Luke standing up for him at dinner—telling him he liked his

jacket—threaded warmly through his veins. Gave him this weird, hopeful feeling. Like maybe . . . maybe Luke wouldn't be like any of the past guys he'd dated.

He wanted to take tonight as proof they could be something, but doubt nagged in his mind.

He heard the echo of Luke's laughter . . . remembered that first scathing look.

Nico was too scared about being wrong. His trust had been broken one too many times. His heart couldn't take it.

Especially not with Luke. Especially not with the way Nico was falling for him.

Especially not since Luke still used Nico as a fake boyfriend to make his ex jealous.

But . . . damn it. He loved this flirting. Loved their chemistry in bed together. Loved living with him . . .

Nico needed to tread with caution.

And maybe he needed to expose the true Nico and see how long Luke hung around then.

Nico ran his finger around the lip of his wine glass. "Do you have plans next Friday night?"

Luke's bewildered expression turned Nico's stomach. "Are you calling in your favor?"

"No," Nico said, his hand trembling as he sipped his wine. "Isaiah and his boyfriend, Darren, are performing at a charity event at Darren's childhood house. It's to raise money for children's cancer research."

"That's admirable."

"Yeah, and Isaiah is an amazing pianist. Darren agreed to play if Isaiah would. He plays saxophone and banjo."

"Banjo?" Luke snorted. "Really?"

"Evidently he had dreams of being a Mummer before someone reminded him he had to run the company one day. Anyway, I got comped two tickets. Isaiah and Darren know we're not a couple. So we could go as friends."

"Friends." Luke nodded slowly.

Nico pinched the stem of his glass, ignoring how his stomach fluttered seeing Luke's disappointment with the label.

Nico needed to be *sure*. Really, really sure. The sureist.

"It could be good fun? It's a black-tie event, so we get to dress up."

Luke eyed Nico's sports jacket, and his eyes hit Nico's warmly. "Dress up?"

"Is that a yes?"

Nico: Here. Holy Shit Chateau Gage is HUGE!

Isaiah: Ha! I'll have Darren come find you.

NICO COULDN'T STOP EYING the way the sleek black tux hugged Luke perfectly. "You look great," Nico murmured absently.

They were moving up a grand path toward a lit mansion, pockets of finely dressed elite ahead of them.

Luke adjusted his coat, flashing him a grin. "Good thing Rocco 'knew a guy' who could hook us up at the last minute."

Nico snorted. "What can I say? We take care of our own."

Luke's gaze swept over Nico and his smile radiated. "I didn't think you could look any hotter than you did last weekend, but I was wrong. Aaaand, I probably shouldn't have said that. There won't be enough room in the mansion for your big head."

Nico scoffed, but his stomach twisted.

Luke gestured to the ground. "They even have a red carpet for you to walk."

"Actually, dahling, I think it was put out for you." Nico tensed, waiting for Luke's response—

Luke grabbed Nico's hand and tugged him close. He spoke low in his ear, almost tutting. "You don't take compliments well."

Nico shivered, and Luke's warm hand pumped his twice before letting go.

Darren's parents greeted them at the door. Nico had met them at one of Darren's soccer games. When he first met Darren, Isaiah had been hopeless when it came to soccer. Much like Nico was with baseball. He'd been Isaiah's 'beard', chatting with the Gages about the game.

When Mrs. Gage saw them, her face lit up. "Oh, my!" She fanned her face, and Nico remembered how much he'd loved her company.

"You look amazing, Mrs. Gage."

"I know I told you to call me Peg," she said, hugging him.

"And I know I told you that would never happen." He inched to his right, bringing Luke forward.

Mrs. Gage cut across him, eagerly. "You must be Nico's boyfriend." She gave him a hug.

To his credit, Luke didn't let her pronouncement faze him, and he returned the embrace.

He laughed nervously, and they shuffled along to allow the hosts to meet their other guests.

Inside, Luke reached for Nico's hand again. Perhaps Luke thought they were back to faking for the night?

Nico could've told him otherwise.

Should've.

But, fuck, it felt too nice.

He searched for Isaiah as he and Luke took in the grandeur of the Gages' home.

"Nico!"

He turned just in time for Isaiah's bear hug.

"I missed you," Isaiah said when he let go. His gaze darted to their still-joined hands before he looked up, a dozen questions sparking his eyes. "Nice to finally meet you."

"Likewise. Nico texts you so often, I feel like you live with us."

Isaiah's gaze kept dropping to their hands. "I think I might have missed a few texts."

Nico eyed him hard, silently begging him to drop it. "Later," he mouthed, and Isaiah grinned and let it go.

"Enjoy the show; we'll catch up after."

Nico

Isaiah: What are you doing tomorrow? Darren wants to go out before I go home Sunday.

Nico: Can't. Luke's company picnic is tomorrow.

Isaiah: You still pretending you're pretending to be boyfriends?

Nico: We're not boyfriends.

NICO GROWLED, frustrated as much with himself as with Isaiah. Of course people thought they were dating; whenever they went out together, they played fake boyfriends. And then they came home to eat their meals together and sleep in the same bed.

And even after a week of ramping up his flair for the dramatic, Luke still smiled at him brightly. Hell, maybe even *more* brightly.

Those smiles were screwing with him. Made him so close to admitting he wanted to drop the fake boyfriend act and do the true boyfriend act.

Except.

Luke still asked him to attend company things to make Kent jealous.

He poked a fork into his cold lemon chicken. The green beans and rice were cold now too. Cold like his appetite.

He'd cleared away Luke's place setting. No sense having it out when he had to stay late to deal with some Kent nonsense.

At least he'd texted to say he wouldn't be home for dinner.

Another bite, and his stomach revolted. He couldn't eat anymore.

The hand-holding business and snuggling at nights . . . *those smiles.*

Luke *acted* like he wanted Nico, but he couldn't wean himself away from his ex.

If only Nico could pull back, become more detached . . .

If only pigs could fly.

Tomorrow he was expected to don a happy face and put on a show again. Part of him wanted to, because he was addicted to imagining what it would be like for real. The other part told him to go out with Isaiah and Darren. Stop setting his heart up for another beating.

Nico wrapped up the food and stared at the pans. When Luke cleaned, Nico didn't mind helping. It didn't feel like a chore. Alone, it sucked. With each pan he set out to dry, the hope that Luke would get home before he finished dimmed.

Was Luke enjoying dinner with Kent tonight?

Fuck.

The last pot clean, Nico dried his hands on the dishtowel. Growing up, there was always someone around. Loud, noisy, demonstrative family. Without Luke, the silent apartment left him anxious.

He took a quick shower and readied himself for bed.

At nine forty-five. On a Friday night.

He rarely went to bed this early on a weekday, but on a weekend? Fuhgeddaboudit.

Nico flopped back onto his pillow and lay there in the silence of their apartment.

What was wrong with him? Normally he was good at bottling

his feelings. Those who weren't available, were unattainable, or didn't want him, he simply left alone.

Then Luke bowled into his life.

Nico rolled over and stared at Luke's empty space in the bed. The stupid bed they shared.

"Stupid fucking Amazon." If they'd had the mattress, they'd never have crossed the line. Nico would never have known how intensely compatible they were.

And he would not be fretting about play-acting Luke's boyfriend—*again*—at the picnic tomorrow.

CHAPTER FOURTEEN

Luke

Luke: Nico's acting weird today.

Coury: Can't imagine why.

Luke: You're not helping.

Coury: Maybe if you told him you're not faking anymore it might help.

Luke stood in the shade of a large oak tree, watching his colleagues clumped together eating, drinking, schmoozing, flute glasses in their hands. Less like a picnic and more like Sunday brunch outside. Or a cocktail party with food.

Breezes washed over his face. Fresh, but not fresh enough to clear his pounding head. He leaned against the knotty tree trunk and grumbled at his phone. At Coury's messages.

Coury was right. Luke wasn't faking it anymore. Hadn't been for a while.

The guy pushed every one of Luke's buttons. Every. Damn. One.

Problem was, every time he thought he and Nico were getting closer, Nico pulled back. Since the charity event, he'd distanced himself even more.

Nico might have spent the day smiling and tossing out quick comebacks but there was a rigidness to his expressions, his posture.

Had Luke's forthrightness made Nico uneasy? Did Nico know how Luke felt? Was he letting him down quietly?

Or was Nico still processing it? Still deciding what *he* wanted?

God, Luke just wanted to haul him aside and talk through this.

But he got it. Living together made things awkward. Nonverbal communication kept everyone's pride intact.

Sure, Luke would love it if they talked and Nico said he was into him too.

But what if Nico rejected him? He'd be mortified. He'd have to live with Nico and accept his worst fear that he was too boring for anything serious.

Nico curved around a picnic blanket, two wineglasses in his hand. He smiled as he approached and passed Luke a drink. "Not sure this merlot is as nice as the riesling we had at the game, but it's not bad."

Luke tasted his. He couldn't tell full-bodied from plain old nice. "I got nothing."

"I'm making it my mission to teach you good wine from bad," Nico said easily and then pivoted sharply, frowning into another sip. Like he'd forgotten himself. Luke pinched his wineglass hard, and Nico continued, "I didn't know this was part of Fairmont Park. Not that I'm an expert on Philadelphia parks."

"Me neither." The Lemon Hill Mansion behind them was amazing. "I still can't believe the firm was able to book a museum for our picnic."

"It takes money to maintain historical buildings." Nico spread his arms wide. "I'll bet the security deposit is *huge*."

Luke loved when Nico injected life into the mundane. He made everything more interesting. He made everyone feel welcome. Like they belonged.

Luke swallowed, glancing around the fancy picnic. A far cry from life back home in the Midwest.

Nico leaned against the tree trunk beside him, arms infuriatingly close and not close enough. "Penny for your thoughts?"

"Just wondering if this was the life I wanted." He shrugged.

"Funny how the world expects us to chart our life at an age when science says our decision-making ability isn't fully developed." Nico stared into the crowd. "No wonder 'midlife crisis' is a thing."

"You seem to know what you want."

Nico shook his head. "It's not the same. The bakery comes with my family."

"That's . . ." Pure Nico. "An amazing way to put it."

"It's true. When I'm around them, I'm grounded. I don't want a world without family." Nico never looked over, but he swallowed loudly.

Luke twisted and stared at Nico. "Penny for *your* thoughts."

Nico's fake smile slammed into place, and he grinned at Luke. "I'm wondering if we should brave the line for food yet."

Luke forced down a sigh and held out his hand. "We could both stand to be brave."

The line moved faster than they thought. Luke's plate was piled with flounder in a cream sauce, rice, green beans, and pasta salad. Nothing he'd ever had at a picnic back home. Except the rolls. He took three and extra butter.

They found a table and sat across from each other, Nico constantly scanning the crowds. Halfway through his meal, Nico latched on to something, and his face fell. Luke jerked his head in the direction—

Ah, fuck. Kent and Sebastian had arrived.

"Mind if we join you?" Without waiting for a reply, Kent took the seat next to Luke.

Sebastian's face twitched, but he recovered instantly and set his food on the table next to Nico.

"So, Sebastian." Nico's voice broke the awkward silence, and Luke froze. "My family is staying at your hotel for my sister's wedding."

"Really?" Sebastian smiled, and it seemed to ease the tension. "Which one?"

"Eighteenth and something." Nico shrugged. "It's down near the Ben Franklin Parkway."

"Gotcha. That's the Parkway hotel." He snorted. "I know. So original. When's the wedding?"

"Next weekend. But my parents stayed there last weekend and said it's really nice."

"It was renovated last year." He wiped his mouth. "I'll talk to the GM to be sure they give your family the best rooms."

"I'm sure all the rooms are great, but that's really nice of you."

"Seb's that kind of guy," Kent said, reaching across the table. "Always thinking of others."

Sebastian glared at Kent for a moment, pulled his hand back, and took out his phone. "Give me your contact information, Nico. I'll set up a meeting with the general manager."

Kent tensed next to Luke as their boyfriends exchanged numbers. When Nico and Sebastian put their phones away, Kent nudged Luke. "Some game last night, eh? Harper really crushed those two homers."

What was he up to? "Yeah."

"The bullpens really had to work *overtime* once it got to extra innings."

Luke's gaze darted to Nico, who sat rigid, donning his fakest smile. But even that cracked, and Luke glimpsed a hint of moisture in his eyes.

Fuck.

"I wonder if the other manager flipped a coin before pitching to Harper in the twelfth with two on and one out," Kent continued. "Tough call, you know?"

Nico stood and snatched his glass from the table. "I'm getting a refill. Anyone need anything?"

He walked off before anyone could answer. Sebastian looked between Luke and Kent. "What's that about—"

Luke lurched to his feet, glaring at Kent. "You're such an asshole, you know that? I shouldn't be surprised, given . . ." He swallowed the urge to call Kent a lying, cheating asshole. "Enjoy the rest of the picnic."

He needed to find Nico.

There was no sign of him near the open bar, and he wasn't in the food tent. Luke scrubbed his face. How fucking stupid was he to tell Kent *anything*. From his smarmy tone, it was clear Kent had been waiting for the right time to drop those lines.

"Luke?" He looked up and found Mrs. Umstead across from him. "Something wrong?"

"Just looking for Nico."

"Is everything okay? You look pale."

"A bit too much sun, I think." Good thing he didn't bring his wineglass with him. "You didn't see him, did you?"

She nodded, and Luke's spirits rose. "He went inside the museum. It's cooler there if you need to rest."

He barely said thank you before rushing off. Nico wasn't in the foyer. There were two doorways to choose from. He took the one straight ahead. Three steps in, his shoes squealed against marble as he stopped.

Nico stood bent over an exhibit. Both hands gripped the sides of the plastic case surrounding a model of some building.

"Nico—"

"Don't." It was barely more than a whisper, but it struck Luke right in the gut.

"It's not like you think. Kent twisted my words."

Nico snorted. "You told him what I said."

"I found it endearing. I was telling him what a great guy you are."

Nico held a palm up. "Just forget it. I'm just being overly dramatic. Did you tell him that too?"

"What the hell? No."

Nico kept moving toward the next presentation.

Luke followed, voice growing more desperate, "I told him how before the Phillies game you spent time learning about baseball. That I thought it was sweet of you."

Nico's posture remained stiff, but he didn't squeeze the display case at this stop.

"I know how it looks, but I didn't say it to put you down." And the asshole twisted it around and flung it back at Nico to make him look like a fool. "I should have known better than to confide in him."

Nico's shoulders slumped in defeat. "It's fine."

It wasn't fine.

Nico should yell at him. Tell Luke what an idiot he was for trusting a lying, cheating jerk like Kent.

He inched closer. When Nico didn't move, Luke shuffled closer still.

"Nico?" He tentatively put a hand on Nico's shoulder and closed his eyes.

A hand landed on his and gave it a squeeze. "It's okay. Really."

Luke shifted beside Nico, and when Nico turned, Luke opened his arms.

He expected to be rebuffed, but his heart skipped a beat when Nico slid into the open space between Luke's arms.

"I'm sorry," Luke whispered into the tender embrace.

Nico's breath shuddered over his throat and the crook of his neck. "C'mon. Let's head back."

Relief swelled in this chest.

The idea of losing Nico . . . even though he didn't really 'have' him . . .

God.

Nico

Isaiah: Want to meet for drinks? The six of us are going out later.

Nico: Maybe? Not sure how late this picnic will go.

Isaiah: You're still there with your pretend/not pretend BF?

Nico: Have a safe trip home.

THE PHONE BUZZED with 'Saiah's reply, and Nico shoved it in his pocket without reading. He didn't need to know that 'Saiah was kidding and Nico needed to lighten up.

This needed to stop. Getting upset over the baseball faux pas proved Nico was in too deep already. Friends wouldn't have felt betrayed, they'd have laughed it off. Friends wouldn't have run off because they felt so hurt they might cry.

And there it was.

Emotionally, they *weren't* just friends, but Nico refused to let them be more. He couldn't.

Despite all the shit Kent gave him, some part of Luke still saw good in the guy. Still wished things were different, maybe.

Nico couldn't be a backup boyfriend. Didn't want to play second fiddle. He needed to come first.

At least he knew what being in love felt like. It was fifty feet in front of him with a finger in Kent's face. It didn't take a lip reader to know Luke was standing up for Nico.

Nico scanned the area. No one seemed to be paying attention to Luke and Kent, but he needed to put a stop to their squabble. It wouldn't help Luke if a partner saw them arguing. Curiously, he didn't see Sebastian anywhere. Probably had enough of his 'boyfriend' constantly talking to his ex.

"Luke," Kent whined.

"No!" Luke put his hand up. "Just go away."

Nico steeled his emotions, grabbed Luke's arm, and tugged gently. "C'mon. That's enough. Don't make a scene in front of the partners."

That got their attention and they both looked around to see if anyone was watching. When Kent turned his gaze back to Luke, Nonna would have been proud of the evil eye Nico gave the asshole.

Nico hooked their fingers and made sure Luke followed.

"Thanks for saving me." Luke squeezed their fingers. "I didn't mean for you to have to face him again."

"How about we socialize and then maybe leave?"

"Why? Got a hot date?"

"Sorta."

"Huh?" Luke pulled them to a stop. "You never—"

Nico put his fingers over Luke's lips. "Isaiah asked if *we* would like to join them for drinks later."

Luke's tension ebbed, and Nico couldn't deny he liked seeing it.

Nico shrugged. "I already told him we had this picnic, but maybe after?"

Luke paused before responding. "You want me to ditch this work crowd to hang out with your friends?"

"Yes, and if it's not too much to ask, one other thing?"

Luke chuckled. "Name it."

Nico met his eye. "I don't ever want to see Kent again."

CHAPTER FIFTEEN

Nico

Nico's blood ran hot and fizzy. Wine flowed easily with Isaiah and Darren—as did their conversation. Especially the one where Luke spilled the beans about his first time hooking up with a farm boy.

Adorable, and hot—if only a PG retelling.

They left at midnight, navigating SEPTA, missed their stop, and doubled back.

Laughing, Luke led them up the stairs to their apartment. Nico put a finger to his lips. "Quiet. Mrs. R is sleeping."

His voice echoed off the walls, prompting a louder "shhhh" from Luke. Who promptly tripped over a large, battered box outside their door.

"Holy shit," Luke said. "The air mattress came."

Nico eyed the scuffs and dents. "Bet it won't work." He fumbled to get the key in the lock.

"Sounds like you're hoping it doesn't." Luke scooped up the box and grunted. "Heavy. How did Mrs. R get it up here?"

Nico snickered as he pushed open their door. "She's Wonder Woman in disguise." He twirled around and fell onto their couch.

Laughter filled their apartment, prompting more shushing from Nico.

Luke plunked the box on the floor and staggered. *Lightweight.*

Nico steadied him. "Let's get you to bed."

"Yes, *let's*." He threw his arms around Nico's head and whispered huskily in his ear, warm breath tickling his sensitive neck. "Take me, Nico."

Nico sucked in a breath.

Somewhere in the back of his mind, a warning flashed: *bad idea*. "Luke. You're drunk."

"Tipsy. *Not* wasted." Luke's tongue teased Nico's lobe. "I know exactly what I'm doing."

Nico's body betrayed him with a moan. "This is a bad idea."

Luke tightened his hold and nibbled Nico's neck. "It feels so good with you. How can that be bad?"

Kent. Backup. Second fiddle.

God, those lips did devious things.

His cock pressed achingly hard against Luke's crotch. "It's crossing a line."

"A line we crossed before, and we're still good." Luke grabbed Nico's ass. Tight and firm.

Nico gasped. Yes, but . . .

But . . .

Nico leaned into Luke, canting his hips, reveling in the friction. Luke crushed his lips over Nico's groan.

"You're so fucking hot," Luke whispered between slick, needy kisses. "I want you so bad."

Nico squeezed Luke's nape and fucked his tongue into his pleading mouth. Luke tightened around him, all heat and friction, and they stumbled.

Nico's brain shouted for him to ignore the animalistic lust

pounding through him and pull back. Fall any deeper and he was fucked.

Luke threaded their fingers and led Nico to the bedroom.

Every step, hormones shunted logic to the background.

Just one more night. Just fun.

Then they'd go back to being just friends.

Luke

LUKE WASN'T sure this was a good idea, but he didn't care. Watching Nico with his friends, seeing how much color and sass burst out of him . . . Luke shivered. He'd been half-hard all night. Every sentence, every touch lit Luke's nerve endings.

They were amazing together.

Maybe another round of mind-blowing sex would nudge Nico into the light?

He pulled Nico into a passionate kiss, hands roaming over the hard lines of his sexy body.

He yanked the tails of Nico's shirt from his shorts, slid his hands under his boxers, and massaged Nico's amazing ass.

Nico bucked forward, urgently pushing up Luke's shirt. Luke raised his arms, and Nico broke their kiss, removing the cotton polo. Fingers snapped to his shorts, knuckles massaging his cock as he unbuttoned them. Luke cursed with desire, cupped Nico's face, and plunged his tongue into his hot mouth.

Nico hummed needily and shoved Luke's shorts down. Luke stepped out of the material, flinging them away with his foot.

He gripped Nico's shirt. "Let me—"

"Nope." Gently but firmly Nico pushed him back onto the bed. "Turnabout is fair play. Tonight, I want you naked first."

Tonight. Luke loved the way that sounded like there might be more nights. He scooted onto the mattress, leaned back on his elbows, and cocked his brow. "I hope you enjoy the view as much as I did."

Nico's eyes blazed. He ripped his shirt off and flung it aside. "Fuck, what are you doing to me?"

"Anything you want." *Everything.*

Nico's eyes locked on Luke's with a burning intensity that skittered through Luke's veins like wildfire.

Luke reached into the nightstand and pulled out the lube and condoms he'd stashed there.

Nico ditched his clothes and crawled onto the bed, gloriously naked. He settled his warm, heavy weight atop Luke. "Planning ahead, Mr. DeRosa?"

"Fuck, yeah." He arched wantonly against Nico, cocks rubbing.

Nico shuddered, molding into the thrusts, and Luke looped a leg around the back of Nico's and rolled them.

He smirked down at a flushed Nico.

Nico raised his head, snatching a kiss, hands pulling and kneading Luke's ass. A finger slid between his cheeks and touched his opening. Luke moaned his approval. They were definitely going *there.*

But not yet.

Luke kissed down Nico's body, ran his tongue around the left nipple, and gently bit. Nico cursed and convulsed hard. "Found a spot, did I?"

"You're so evil!" Nico tugged Luke. "Let me torture you a bit."

Luke wriggled free. "You'll get your chance when you fuck me."

His cock twitched at the thought of Nico's thick cock stretching him wide. He sank wet kisses down Nico's chest, tonguing his treasure trail, smiling at every gasp, groan, and thrust.

Luke's chin bumped over Nico's shaft, eliciting some colorful debauched curses. He gripped Nico's hips and sucked the head of Nico's cock into his mouth, slowly inching lower.

Luke pulled off, and Nico's dick flipped against his groin with a smack. "Fuck!"

"We could torture each other simultaneously," Nico said, swinging sideways. He steered Luke's legs around him and engulfed his pulsing-hard cock.

Luke cried out, nerve endings crackling as the head hit the back of Nico's throat.

He rocked into the tight, wet heat, arousal gripping every inch of his body from his curling toes to his fingers that clutched the sheets on either side of Nico's thighs.

Luke lifted Nico's cock, took a deep breath, relaxed his throat, and plunged down. Nico hissed.

"Jesus, Luke. Fuck yeah." Nico devoured Luke's cock, grabbing his ass, burying Luke deeper.

Luke moaned around Nico's length, arms hugging Nico's butt. They were gloriously pressed together, buried in each other's mouths and throats.

Luke bobbed up for air, and quickly plunged down again.

He had to stop, or he'd come. He raised his hips and his dick left Nico's mouth with a wet pop. "Fuck, that feels so good."

"I know." Nico grabbed Luke's shaft and lazily jerked him. "It's one of my favorite things to do."

Would be one of Luke's favorites after tonight. Moving around, he straddled Nico's spit-covered cock and wiggled his ass. "I hope fucking is another favorite."

"Definitely." Nico rocked against him. "Want to start like this? Or do you prefer a different position?"

"I love to ride." Nico's cock throbbed in response to Luke's answer. "But I warn you it makes me come fast."

Nico reached for the supplies Luke had set out. "Want me to pull out as soon as you shoot?"

And there was why he wanted Nico. Concerned more about

Luke than getting off. Most guys he'd been with never asked. "Keep going. I'll let you know when I need you to stop."

He needed him to stop when Nico came.

"Sounds good." Nico stared at the condom and lube. "This might sound weird, but can you put the condom on me while I lube your ass? I know it sounds weird, but I—"

Luke cut him off, crushing their lips together. "Fuck, yeah. That sounds hot."

"Yeah?" Nico's face lit up. "I've always wanted to do this."

Lust filled Nico's gaze. Luke loved the idea that he could give Nico something he'd never done. He plucked the condom from Nico's hand and turned around.

"Go slow?" Kent wasn't small, but he wasn't Nico either. "It's been a while."

"I'll be as gentle as you like."

The lube lid snapped open, and something cool trickled over his hole.

Nico rubbed the flat of his finger over the bajillion nerve endings and teased a finger inside.

Precome pooled onto Nico's pelvis, and he pushed back, eager for more.

Nico snorted. "Or as rough as you like."

"God, Nico. More." Luke hissed as a second caressing finger joined the first. "I want you so bad."

"Suit me up." Nico twisted his fingers, grazing his prostate, and Luke gasped, rutting for more friction.

"I can't see straight with you doing that to me." Closing his eyes, he tore open the foil wrapper.

Liquid flowed down his crack, and Nico's fingers darted in and out of him. "I don't want you even a tiny bit straight."

Luke laughed, muscles clenching around Nico's fingers. "Stop that."

"What? Making you laugh?" Nico rubbed, making Luke's cock jump. "Or this?"

Luke laughed again. "Fucker! Stop torturing me so I can get this damn thing on." He rolled the ring of latex over the glans and pushed it lower with his hand.

"Bossy bottom much?" Nico twirled his fingers back and forth, slipped them out, and pushed the bottle of lube forward. "Can you put some on, please?"

"Now who's bossy?"

Luke poured some lube into his right hand. He coated Nico's cock, smirking when Nico shivered under him.

"The things you do to me, Luke."

Good. Luke *wanted* to do things to him. Wanted Nico to take a chance on him.

Luke tossed the bottle aside and pumped his cock with the excess lube. He really wouldn't last long. Facing Nico, he positioned himself and looked down. Nico fucked Luke with his gaze.

"God, I want you," Luke said.

Nico sat up, eyes locking on Luke's, and pulled him into a kiss.

Luke kissed him back, sinking into the burn as the thick head of Nico's cock pressed into him.

Their kiss hitched when Nico cleared his ring. The burn increased until he was fully impaled. Lips locked together, Luke adjusted to the wonderfully thick cock, *Nico's* wonderfully thick cock, buried deep inside him.

Nico lay patiently, letting Luke dictate their pace. When Luke rose up, he sucked in air and lifted his head.

"Easy." Nico steadied his hands on Luke's hips. "Take it slow."

Luke pulled up until only the head remained inside. "Hell, no." He plunged down hard. "Fuck me, Nico."

Nico tentatively thrust. "Are you sure?"

"I wanna feel you tomorrow when you're not here."

Gripping Luke's hips, Nico guided him up, and when he sank back, Nico rose up, meeting him hard.

"Oh, yeah," Luke whispered huskily. "Give it to me. Fuck me good."

Luke stroked himself.

Nico felt way too good inside him, brushing Luke's prostate with every wild in-stroke.

Panting, Luke closed his eyes, sensation mounting, mounting, mounting as he chased after his orgasm. "I'm gonna come. Kiss me!"

Nico kissed him hard, pistoning in and out of Luke's ass. Luke moaned, and the first shot hit his chin, second, third, and fourth volleys spurting over their torsos.

Nico pushed himself all the way inside and stopped.

"Keep going. It's okay."

"Too late." He grunted. "So hot."

Nico's grip on him relaxed, and Luke pressed a soft kiss on his lips. "God, Nico. That was amazing."

"You're amazing."

They kissed languidly, and Nico pulled back, lazily admiring Luke.

"You quiet types certainly surprise." He skated a ticklish finger through the come on Luke's chest. "You really are a bossy bottom, aren't you?"

Luke nipped a kiss and scrambled to the bathroom for a warm, wet cloth. "When I bottom, I like to get fucked." He cleaned Nico's chest, lips hitching. "But watch out, I top like I bottom."

Nico's smile widened. "That better be a promise."

LUKE WOKE in the middle of the night to a moonlight-drenched room, arm draped over Nico. His hard cock pressed against the cleft of Nico's ass.

Nico pushed back against Luke, squeezing his butt tight around Luke's cock. "I'm so glad you stick to your promises," he said sleepily.

"Mmm?" Luke rocked into the hugging hold of Nico's hot ass cheeks. "You want this inside you?"

Nico burrowed back, tighter, closer. "Fuck yeah."

"Good." Luke nibbled the earlobe by his mouth, eliciting the moan he'd hoped for. "Because I want to be inside you, bad."

He lowered his hand and fisted Nico's cock. Precome leaked over the head, and Luke plied his thumb over the sticky fluid.

Nico gasped, and Luke murmured in his ear, "I need to see your face." Luke rolled on top of Nico, their cocks grinding as he pressed close, eliciting a ragged moan.

Nico wriggled beneath Luke, and fuck, Luke *needed.*

"Oh God, Luke!"

"Like that, did you?"

Nico tried to return the favor, but Luke grabbed his arms and used his weight to keep Nico down.

"Nuh-uh." Luke shook his head and smiled wickedly. "I'm taking care of you right now." He leaned forward and licked the side of Nico's neck.

"Oh, fuck! That's hot."

"Yeah?" Luke shimmied down and blew softly along the side of Nico's stomach. Nico writhed beneath him, and Luke kept inching up his body. He flicked his tongue across a nipple and swirled it around.

A low growl rumbled through Nico's body. Keeping his lips around the small nub, Luke bit gently on the sensitive skin.

"Uhh!" Nico's body arched, and Luke leaned on him, pinning him down.

"So responsive." Luke swiped his tongue along Nico's other side. "Let's see what happens when I move lower."

He inched his way down, dusting Nico's body with light kisses. Nico tensed and sucked in short breaths. Luke's chin touched the tip of Nico's leaking cock, and he raised his head. Shifting slightly, he pushed up on the shaft and swallowed half Nico's dick.

Nico put a hand on Luke's head. "Oh yeah."

Encouraged, Luke ran his lips up and down a few times before his hand dipped lower. His finger brushed over the opening, and Nico shivered.

"Oh, God."

He pulled up and off Nico's cock, but didn't release his hold. "Lube."

Nico twisted to get the supplies, and Luke resumed sucking his cock. He could seriously give Nico head all night and be happy. He loved how it felt and tasted in his mouth.

A bottle touched his shoulder, and without missing a stroke, Luke took the lube and popped the top. He squeezed the slippery liquid and ran a slick, teasing finger around Nico's hole.

Luke dipped inside.

Nico shifted, pushing down eagerly on Luke's finger. "Oh fuck yeah."

The need in Nico's voice was a huge turn-on. Luke slid his finger in and out a couple of times before adding the second. He twirled his fingers back and forth as he moved in and out.

Nico grunted. "Luke. Fuck me. Please."

Luke stopped sucking and looked up. "Bossy bottom much?"

"Only when I don't get what I want." Nico tore open the condom and held it up. "Can I?"

"Fuck, yeah." Luke got to his knees, his cock at full mast, and inched forward.

Nico's warm hands rolled the condom down. "Can we do this face-to-face?"

Luke lubed his pulsing length. "Yeah?"

"I want . . . I want to watch you while you fuck me."

"So hot." Luke dipped and snagged Nico into a passionate, tongue-twisting kiss.

"*Ti amo tantissimo*," Nico said, pulling back for air.

Luke kissed him again. "Whatever you said sounded sexy as fuck."

Nico swallowed hard.

Luke raised Nico's legs and kissed the right calf as he positioned himself for entry.

Watching for signs Nico was in pain, Luke kept up a slow pressure. Nico winced, and Luke paused.

Nico clasped Luke's butt. "Don't stop."

The words said go, but Nico's face said pain. "Nico, I don't want to hurt you."

"You won't." He huffed through the obvious pain. "It's been a few years."

"Years?" Luke stopped.

"Four." Nico reached up to pull Luke down and nipped at his ear. His words skittered warmly over his earlobe. "Don't stop. I'll be fine once I get used to you."

Luke carefully finished his entry. Nico gripped him tight and hot. God, he'd had sex before, but he'd never felt so connected.

Nico grabbed Luke's head and pressed their lips together. After a deep kiss, he moved back. "Fuck me, Luke. Like you promised."

He pulled back slowly and plunged forward, eliciting a deep moan. The pain was gone; this was pleasure.

Gaze fixed on Nico, Luke didn't rush his strokes. When he pulled back, he angled so his cock rubbed Nico's prostate. Nico's eyes rolled back.

"*Fuuuucck*."

"Like that?"

"So much." Nico opened his eyes. "Harder. I need more. Please."

Having begun with long, deep thrusts, Luke moved to shorter, faster, harder ones. Nico's ragged breathing and demands for more spurred Luke on.

Luke gulped air as he neared release. Beneath him, Nico grabbed his cock and stroked fast. Keeping his rhythm, Luke was so close when Nico grunted.

The muscles surrounding Luke's cock contracted as a volley of come hit Nico in the face. His body kept spasming, and Luke lost it. He shoved in fast and hard and kept himself buried inside Nico as he came. After a couple of shots, he pounded a few more strokes to finish his orgasm.

Beyond happy, he collapsed onto Nico, who wrapped his arms around Luke and hugged him tight. They remained still until their breathing almost returned to normal.

Luke propped himself on his elbows and looked down. He remained inside Nico, not ready to withdraw.

"Four years? You should have told me."

"I didn't want you to stop."

"God, Nico. I thought you *liked* bottoming."

Nico cradled Luke's face and their gazes met tenderly. "I do. I just haven't met anyone I wanted to do that with in a long time."

Luke's chest seized. "And you wanted to with me?"

Nico broke his gaze, his Adam's apple jutting. "You're careful. You feel safe. I wanted to *practice* again."

Luke rested his forehead against Nico's temple. "You feel amazing, Nico."

Nico chuckled. "It was good for you? I don't think I've ever come so hard."

Luke's cock slipped out of Nico, and he felt Nico's shiver. "It was everything for me, Nico. Now let's clean up. I'm impatient to get to the next good part."

"What's that?"

"Spooning you."

CHAPTER SIXTEEN

Nico

Nico blinked in the early morning light. His left arm was asleep, and Luke was using his chest as a pillow. He wrapped his arm around Luke's shoulder, pulling his sleeping body closer. Luke's soft breathing played across Nico's bare torso. He shivered, as much from the air as from replaying last night.

His phone buzzed. Nico glanced at the side table and groaned. Shit.

He shifted and Luke stirred. "Huh? What?"

"I have to go to work. Vito is still sick, and they're in a bind. Wish I could call in."

Luke rolled off Nico, the outline of Nico's morning wood tenting the thin sheet. "I think I know how much you want to call in. I'm not going anywhere. We can wash, rinse, and repeat tonight."

Nico smirked as he rubbed his abs. "Speaking of washing, I should shower."

"Why? I think smelling like sex would be hot. Pheromones are a thing. You'd have a line ten deep all morning."

Nico waggled his eyebrows at Luke. "Good point. Then all of Philly's hot guys will flock to me."

Luke rolled out of bed like fire ants had crawled in. His cock stood straight up. "Right. In the shower you go. I'll join you to make sure every pheromone is licked—scrubbed clean."

Nico's dick twitched. "I don't think that's a good idea. I'll be late."

Luke glanced at their clock. "Please don't tell me this is an excuse because you hate shower sex."

"What? No! If anything, it's because I like it too much. Well, the *idea* of it at least. I've never showered with anyone before."

"Really? We definitely need to fix that." Luke stepped into his boxers. "Not right now, but soon."

"Promises, promises." Nico winked and walked into their bathroom.

If they got started again, Nico wasn't sure he'd make it to work. He turned the water on and peed while it got warm. Once he pulled the shower curtain back, he said, "If you need to come in, you can."

"Thanks, I need to pee like a racehorse."

Not that Nico had been listening, but Luke hadn't been kidding about needing to go. He did his best to ignore Luke standing inches beyond the opaque curtain and worked the shampoo into his hair.

"I wish we had more time. Kent hated shower sex. He refused to even try it."

Nico's spirits sank at Kent's name. Everything still came back to that guy.

"Maybe you'll need a shower when you get back from work."

Nico forced a playful lilt to his voice, but it only served to deepen the ache. "Maybe, but I'm helping E unpack today. I might be home late."

"Oh, right. What time are you going to be back?"

"If it gets late, I'll probably crash there and be home

tomorrow morning." Nico scrubbed the soap from his hair. That came out harsher than he meant. "We'll see. Hopefully, I'll be back tonight."

"Yeah, hopefully."

Luke shut the door, and Nico's heart screamed in pain. He'd needed to do it, but he hated hurting Luke. No matter how close they got, he still clung to Kent. It was too much for Nico to take that risk.

Elisa: At the condo. You still coming to help?

Nico: Of course. Text me the address.

NICO WALKED up Delancy Place looking for his sister's building. He still hadn't gotten over the guilt of leaving after Estelle asked him to stay longer. When he told her he couldn't, the lengthy pause told him she'd expected he'd stay and didn't have a backup plan. Her, "That's okay, hon. You were great to help us as much as you did," didn't make it better.

Part of it was his fault; he'd let them take advantage of him. Something Luke reminded him of every time he agreed to an additional shift or stayed late. Shit. *Luke.*

He'd done so well all morning pushing Luke from his thoughts. Why'd he have to slip right before he got to Elisa's place?

Counting the numbers, he stopped in front of her building. It was an enormous old rowhome, converted into condos. Elisa and Elliott bought the middle unit.

"Swanky," he said.

He vaulted up the steps and rang the buzzer.

"Hello?"

"Hey, E. It's me."

The buzzer let him in, and he took the stairs two at a time.

Elisa opened the door just as he got to the second floor. "This looks nice."

"It is." Her excitement matched her smile. "Come in and let me show you around."

The tour took less than three minutes, but the place had charm. "I like it."

"We do too." She led them to a small table and chairs in the kitchen. "Did you ask Luke to the wedding yet?"

This was so wrong. "I thought you wanted me to help you unpack, not to interrogate me about my love life."

"Since when can't you walk and talk?"

"I can, but I don't want to talk about it."

"That means you didn't ask him," She shook her head and frowned at him. "Boo, you have to bring him."

"I can't." He wouldn't.

"If you don't, Nonna is gonna fuss."

"Pffft. You're crazy. This is *your* wedding. She won't even notice."

"Now you're being delusional. After how he took down Elliott's mom at dinner, Nonna is convinced you two are next to get married."

"That's ridiculous. Even if that's true, it'll pass."

"No, boo. It won't. She's gonna stress over it."

"She'll get over it." He couldn't keep faking it to keep her happy. "I'll tell her we broke up."

"Please don't do that." She stared at the table and exhaled. "You've been Nonna's 'dear boy' since you opened your eyes. I don't want her sad on my wedding day. Please ask him?"

"C'mon, E. Don't do this."

"Why not? You guys are so good together."

More than she knew. "He's not . . . he's still in love with his ex."

"That's such crap, boo."

"No, it's not. It's the truth." Nico had talked to E about everything, but this time he struggled. "I mean, this morning, we were talking about . . . stuff—"

"Talking about how you two had sex last night." She rolled her eyes as if talking about him and Luke having sex wasn't awkward for him. "Go on."

"We were talking about *stuff,* and he brings up Kent. Talk about ice water on a mood."

Elisa made a face as she mulled over what he'd said. The fact she didn't immediately say he was crazy told him all he needed to know.

"See? It's a problem. And every time Kent calls, Luke runs off to help. I mean, come on. The asshat cheated on him. If that isn't reason enough to tell him to fuck off, nothing is."

"You need to tell him how you feel."

"Right." Nico rolled his eyes. "I can start by singing 'Feelings' first."

She smacked his arm. "Don't be such a troglodyte. I'm serious."

"I am too. I'm not going to tell him I want to discuss my fears."

"Why not? Afraid?"

Nico fixed her a look. "Yes. That's why they're called *fears.*"

"You're being silly." She held up a finger to cut off his protest. "You are. Not talking to him guarantees you lose him."

"It's not that simple. I'm sure he likes me." After last night he was positive of that. "The problem, as I keep saying, is he's still in love with his ex. He may not realize it over the hurt and anger, but he is. I can't compete with that."

"Can't or won't?"

Nico went to the window and watched someone try to fit an SUV into a parking space just big enough for a Mini. Elisa kept silent, and he knew she could keep quiet until he answered. "Can't. How do you compete with an idea?"

"By being better than the idea." Her chair scraped on the floor. "Boo, I tell you this all the time, but you are the most amazing person. Luke sees that. What are you so afraid of?"

Anyone but his sister and he could get away with lying, but she knew him too well. "I don't know. Kent . . . he's jealous of me. I have a feeling he's angling to get back with Luke. It'll break my heart if he picks Kent over me."

"You don't know that will happen."

"The risk is too much. It fucking hurt when Tomas left me, okay? And Tomas . . . hell, he's *nothing* compared to Luke."

She came up behind him and wrapped her arms around his waist. "My advice is to talk to him. Yeah, I know what you're going to say, but it's the only way to approach this. Ask him if he sees a future for you two."

"I'm not sure that's a good idea. Things could get awkward. We still have to live together."

"Boo, things already are awkward."

He swallowed the protests he had ready.

"What do you have to lose?" she whispered.

Only everything. But she was right. Better to kill any lingering hope he and Luke would be together than to continue with this mood-crushing uncertainty.

Luke

LUKE TURNED LEFT on Pine Street and headed home. The entire day had been a blur. After their amazing night, the morning's tub of ice water had left him in a funk all day. If they'd asked him what he did all day, he might not have remembered.

"Hey, Luke."

His head popped up, and he found Nico sitting on the stoop with a goofy grin.

"Nico? What are you doing there?"

"Waiting for you." His playful mood disappeared. "Can we talk?"

Luke had planned to ask Nico the same thing, but hearing those three words come from Nico scared him. "Sure."

Pushing up, Nico led them upstairs. "I didn't have time to cook. Do you want to go somewhere or order takeout?"

Suggesting they go out to eat calmed Luke a bit. Nico wouldn't suggest that if their talk was going to cause a problem. "Either is good."

"I vote we go out. There's a sushi bar near Front Street I've wanted to try all summer."

"Sushi it is."

"Great." Nico unlocked the door and let Luke go in first. "Do you want to change?"

"Not really." He avoided Nico's gaze. "I've kinda wanted to talk too, so let's do that first."

"Right." Nico sat on one end of the futon and tucked a leg under him. "So, the thing is, I like you, Luke. A lot."

It felt good to finally hear that from him. Only, Nico didn't seem happy. "But . . .?"

"Kent."

"Kent what?"

Nico breathed deeply and then exhaled. "I'm afraid you'll go back to him."

"Nico, that's crazy. Why would I go back to a lying, cheating asshole?"

"I don't know, but every time he calls or texts, you rush to answer. Every time he needs something, you help him." He shrugged. "You say you don't like him, but you act like you still do."

He opened his mouth to deny it, but Nico's sad eyes stopped his words. A simple denial wasn't going to ease Nico's fears.

"What did I say this morning that has you so worried?"

Nico's shoulders slumped in defeat. "It's nothing."

"It's *something*." Luke took Nico's hands in his. "Nico, I'm tired of *pretending* we're going out. This weekend, last night, I wasn't pretending. I didn't ask you to the picnic just to have a date. I asked you because I wanted you to go with me.

"Last night I didn't just want to get off, I wanted to be that close with you. I know you feel the same way, but I keep giving you a reason to hold back. I need to fix that so you'll trust me when I say I don't want Kent. I want you."

"I trust you, Luke."

"Then please tell me what I said that . . ." Of course. He squeezed Nico's fingers. "We were talking about us and I mentioned him, didn't I?"

Nico nodded. "I know it's not rational, but it feels like he's there every time we do something."

"I see." He thought back on all their dates. Kent—or Kent's name—popped up too often to count.

Nico pulled his hands back, and Luke tightened his grip. "I guess I'm pissed at myself that I didn't see what I was doing. I've been wondering all summer what I needed to do to get you to stop pushing me away."

Nico finally looked up. His expression was guarded, but not skeptical. "I probably should have said something sooner. It's just, it scared me how much I liked you. After what happened with Tomas, I was trying to . . . you know . . ."

"Protect yourself?"

"Yeah."

Luke inched closer. "I realize that to you, every time I helped him it looked like I wasn't over him. But trust me, I am."

"I do."

Luke noticed Nico's clothes. He'd changed out of his Esposito's shirt and wore a tight, shiny black collared one. "I like that shirt on you."

"Really?" He freed his hand and ran it over the fabric. "I figured I'd wear it to dinner. If it's not too much"

"No, it's perfect." He pulled the hand he still held too his lips. "It took me a long time to figure out why you kept wearing plain T-shirts, when the first times I saw you, you were full of color. Your confidence had been knocked. You didn't trust yourself—trust the world—that you could be true to yourself."

"People always say I'm too much. But I *like* bright clothes, and I can be a bit . . . big, sometimes."

"You mean huge." Luke cupped the back of Nico's head and brought their foreheads together. "That makes you, *you*, Nico. I wouldn't change it for the world."

Nico hiccupped. "All this pretending, Luke? I really wanted it to be real."

"It was. For most of summer, I was pretending to pretend."

"Since when?"

Luke wiggled his head but didn't break the contact. "You had me at our first kiss."

"We spent the *whole* summer pretending? That's when I fell for you too."

"Only you pushed me away."

"I was scared."

"I know."

Luke put both hands on Nico's cheeks "To be clear, all those *favors* were fake. I was asking you out every time."

"And even though I was worried, I still couldn't say no." He put his hands over Luke's, sending a charge through Luke's body.

Unable to hold back, he kissed Nico. "Inviting me to the fund-raiser gave me crazy hope. It wasn't for convenience. It wasn't to pretend to anyone. You wanted *me* there."

Nico laughed and shook his head. "I can't believe we wasted the last seven weeks."

"Did we?" Luke arched a brow. "We went out on a bunch of dates. We ate dinner together practically every day. Every night, we slept in the same bed. I couldn't have scripted a better summer if I tried."

"When you put it like that."

"How would you put it?" Luke rubbed their noses together.

"Just like you said." Nico kissed him, and the contact riddled through him from his feet to the hair at his nape. "Best summer ever."

Luke slanted those warm, soft lips over his. Arms came around him, clutching him tight, and Nico kissed Luke back with the same urgency and need.

"Come on." Luke rose from the futon. "Let me change, and let's go have a real, not-pretending-to-pretend first date."

Nico got up but didn't let Luke get away. "Luke?"

"Yeah?"

"I still don't want to see Kent again," Nico whispered.

"You won't." Luke kissed his forehead. "I promise. You won't."

CHAPTER SEVENTEEN

Luke

Luke: You at the bakery?

Nico: Nope. Helping E with wedding stuff.

Luke: Will you be home tonight?

Nico: Sure will. Anything you want for dinner?

Luke: Just you.

Should he send a silly emoji to make it seem less desperate? Or would that come across like he *didn't* want to see Nico? "Ugh!"

"Everything okay, Luke?"

He dropped his phone as he looked up. Chris Rayner leaned against the doorframe and stared into Luke's tiny office.

"Chris!" He looked down for his phone, and then back up, cheeks burning. "I was just texting Nico."

"Calm down." Chris stepped inside and shut the door. "You're allowed to text people. No one expects you'll work every second you're here."

"Okay."

"Is everything all right?" He sat in the lone chair in Luke's tiny office. "I was walking by and heard you."

"Yeah. Everything's fine. Thanks." He kept his gaze on Chris as he reached down to retrieve his phone. "Nico is swamped with wedding stuff. His sister is getting married on Saturday."

"Ah." Chris smiled and sat back. "Speaking of Nico, I want to thank you and him for playing with the kids on Sunday. Linda and I appreciated it."

"Like that was a chore." Nico especially enjoyed it. "They're great kids. If that doesn't sound too suck-upish."

Chris laughed and shook his head. "Not from you. The whole ride home it was 'Nico showed me this awesome soccer move,' or 'Luke helped me fly like Superman,' or my favorite, 'Nico taught me to waltz.' I think my daughter has her first crush at age eight."

"That could be . . ." He shrugged. "Awkward?"

"You're telling me. Aside from the fact I'm so not ready to deal with my daughter dating, she's eight, he's in college, *and* he's your boyfriend. Pierce, my ten-year-old, knew you two are boyfriends and tried to explain it to her. She, however, refused to accept Nico wasn't meant to be her prom date."

They laughed, and Luke finally relaxed. "Seriously, it was fun playing with them. Nico started playing soccer with Pierce, and Nicholas was upset because he couldn't play with the big kids, so I asked him if he wanted to fly like Superman. Evidently he thinks Nico is just a really big kid."

"All three of my children think he's one of the kids."

"When Bonnie felt left out, Nico offered to dance with her." Luke smiled at how easily Nico had gotten down on a knee to be at eye level with Bonnie and asked her to dance with him.

"From what I could tell, she stood on his feet and he did all the dancing. I hope his feet are okay."

Luke chuckled. "They're fine. He's the one who told her to stand there."

"Either way, it was nice of both of you to entertain them. They were *not* happy they had to come to some 'old people party,' as Pierce called it. You two made it a fun time. So thank you."

"You're welcome." Even though it wasn't a big deal, Luke remembered what his father said about compliments: always acknowledge them.

"Well, that was all I came by to say. Maybe before the summer is over, you two can come to the house for dinner."

"Sure. I'll talk to Nico about it." Now that they weren't faking it anymore. "Thank you."

"My pleasure." He opened the door and then turned around, grinning. "Just be warned, the kids are going to think you're there to see them."

Luke snorted. "Right. I'll keep it in mind."

His screensaver—a picture from the Phillies game—had kicked in while he'd talked to Chris. The selfie of him and Nico with the game in the background had been a lark. Something to prove to Isaiah that Nico actually went to the game. They had their arms around each other, and despite their date being an act, they looked happy. *Because we were happy.*

His phone buzzed, and Luke froze. How would Nico react to his "just you" comment? He turned the phone over and frowned.

Kent: I need to talk to you. It's important.

Right. It was never important.

Luke typed and then stopped. Why engage him? After the overtime/coin flip comment at the picnic, he didn't see any point in further communication. The more he thought about it, the madder it made him.

Tapping his phone, Luke blocked him.

He should have done that when he heard Sebastian say they'd been dating for three months. It felt liberating. Like the weight around his waist had been removed. He set the phone down and returned to the project he'd been working on.

The phone rattled on his desk, and he turned it over, half expecting another Kent text.

Nico: You had me at hello.

Luke's heart flipped as he smiled at the screen.

Luke: Do you even know where that came from?

Leave it to Nico to pull all the right strings. He stared at his phone as Nico typed.

Nico: That sports movie, with Tom McGuire.

He laughed so loud, he watched the door for people to come check him out.

Luke: Actually, it was Jerry Cruise.

Worried that Chris might swing by and see him still texting, he put the phone in his lap and tried to focus on his work. That proved nearly impossible as he tried to anticipate Nico's comeback.

After he'd read the same paragraph for the fourth time, Nico's response appeared.

Nico: Whatever. Can we agree it was that romance movie jocks could pretend they were going to see for the sports?

Luke exercised more restraint this time and merely snickered.

Luke: OMG! I remember thinking that exact thought when I saw it.

Luke: As for dinner, whatever you're making is fine.

Nico: Okay great. I'll make bologna sandwiches.

He loved the easy banter between them. Nico wouldn't eat bologna if it was the only thing in the fridge.

Luke: Use spicy mustard please.

Someone walked by his office, and Luke realized he'd gotten nothing done. "Okay. No more texting," he whispered to his phone.

An email notice popped up on his screen. From Kent. Because the world wanted to torture him.

Subject: Really Important!

Seb broke up with me and told me to leave the apartment. I need to crash with you for a day or two. Please?

Was he fucking kidding? In what universe did that happen?

No, you can't crash at our place. Nico doesn't want you around. Find a hotel.

Luke's phone buzzed. "Jesus fucking Christ." His head shot up to check his door. When no one walked by, he checked his screen.

Coury: Hey, bro. How's it going?

Luke: Got time to talk?

He held the phone expectantly and was rewarded when Coury's name appeared.

"Hey, Coury. Thanks for making time for me."

"As if. So, what's up?" Coury paused, but before Luke could answer, he added, "Or should I guess this has to do with Nico?"

"Sorta. It's Kent, which kinda means it involves Nico. But not really."

"Wow. Philadelphia is really improving your communication skills."

"C'mon. I'm serious." Normally he was good goofing with Coury, but not right then. "You were right."

"I usually am." If it wasn't true, Luke would have told him to fuck off. "What was I right about?"

"Sebastian broke up with Kent."

"Too bad I didn't bet you. You'd have to pay me whatever I wanted."

Ha! "Kent asked if he could crash at our place for a night or two."

"Are you shitting me? That's some fucking balls."

"Right?"

"You didn't say yes, did you?"

Clearly his roommate saw him as a total pushover. "Of course not. Nico told me the reason he's been holding back all summer is he's afraid I'll go back to Kent."

"As if you'd take that ass-munch back."

"Yeah, I can't believe I dated him in the first place." Luke paused when he thought someone was coming. No one walked by. "Nico doesn't want Kent around."

"Can't blame him for that."

"Nope, me neither. I promised him he wouldn't have to see Kent again. Which is why Kent absolutely can't stay at my place."

"Luke, even if you hadn't promised Nico, he absolutely shouldn't stay at your place."

"I know." This time he definitely heard someone. "Hang on."

Before he'd turned round, Kent walked in. "Luke. Can I talk to you?"

"I'm on the phone." He tried to shoo Kent out of the room, but the asshole walked further into the small office.

"I know, but this is important. I really need to talk to you. Please."

"Hang on, Coury." He held the phone against his chest. "I said no. Now will you *leave*? I'm busy."

"Yeah, talking to your roommate is such a work-related activity." He pulled back the chair and sat. "I'll wait until you're done with your personal call."

"As if you're here to discuss work. Go wait in your office."

"I'll wait *here*."

Gritting his teeth, Luke shook his head. "Fine." He freed the phone. "I'll call you in a few, Coury. I need to get outside."

"Sure."

Luke snagged his badge off the desk without looking at Kent. He stopped at the door. "If you're here when I get back, I'm calling security."

A STOMACH-RUMBLING aroma met Luke halfway up the stairs. Whatever Nico was making smelled amazing. He smiled, thinking of Nico at the stove, cooking something Nonna taught him. Making dinner for them.

A wave of new deliciousness struck him as Luke pushed the door open. Luke was sure he'd never had it before.

"Honey, I'm—" He stopped in the doorway. "Home."

Nico stood in the living room pounding out something on his phone. The real shock, however, was Kent. Sitting on the couch with his bags at his feet.

"I asked for one thing," Nico whispered. "I thought you promised."

"Nico . . ." Luke's head whipped toward Kent. "What are you doing here?"

"You said I could stay here for a couple of nights." The nasty smirk slammed into Luke like a gut punch. "Sorry if I got here before you could talk to Nico."

"The fuck? I told you . . ." He turned back to Nico. "I told him *no*."

"*Really*?" Nico looked on the verge of tears. "You break your word and then you lie about it?"

"Nico—"

"I have the emails, Luke! Kent forwarded them to me." He tapped his finger hard on the phone screen. "You told him you'd talk to me and it would be okay for him to stay."

"Nico, I—" His phone pinged, and he looked down. An email from Nico.

"What the fuck is this?"

From: Kent

To: Luke

Seb broke up with me. Can I crash at your place for a couple of nights?

~ ~ ~

From: Luke

To: Kent

Sorry to hear it. Yeah, you can crash at the apartment.

~ ~ ~

From: Kent

To: Luke

You sure it's okay with Nico?

~ ~ ~

From: Luke

To: Kent

I'll talk to him. I'm sure it will be fine.

~ ~ ~

He read the emails three times before he looked up. "I didn't write these."

Nico had been watching him but turned away as soon as Luke looked up. His expression broke Luke's heart.

"That's it?" He stepped into his shoes. "You didn't write them?"

Luke looked at Kent, but before he could answer, Nico walked past him.

"I expected better from you." Nico opened the door. "On so many levels."

He walked out of the apartment and shut the door, hard.

"Nico! Wait." Luke put his phone on the table by the door and reached for the handle. Kent grabbed his arm before he could open the door.

When Luke turned, Kent had his bag over his shoulder. "I've changed my mind. I'll get a hotel room. You two have some issues to work out."

He stepped in front of Luke, blocking the stairs.

"Move!"

Kent continued to walk down slowly.

"Move, dammit, or I'll shove you out of my way."

Kent backed against the wall and gestured for Luke to go first.

Thumping down the stairs, Luke burst out the front door. "Nico!"

He searched left and right, but no Nico. Where did he go? How could he have disappeared so fast?

Kent brushed past. "Guess I'm not the only one who's single again."

Luke reached for his phone, but of course he'd left it upstairs. Racing back to their apartment, he grabbed his phone. The call went straight to voicemail.

"Fuck!" He pounded out a text. When he hit send, he waited, but it didn't show as delivered. "Fuck! Fuck! Fuck!"

How did Nico get away so fast? Never mind that, where would he go? Pushing everything else aside, he focused on what Nico would do. The bakery was closed. He wasn't here. That left . . .

Luke: Hey Elisa. I'm worried about Nico. My ex surprised us right as we were gonna eat and N ran out. If you hear from N, let me know please?

Thank God Elisa knew the truth about them. Except . . . where the fuck did those emails come from?

He opened the email from Nico and scanned the headings. They came from his work email account. But how? He never sent those. Kent must have doctored them.

Checking again, he saw the time, 11:10 a.m. Pulling up his phone list, he saw the call from Coury at 11:03. He returned the call at 11:09, right after Kent . . .

"Son of a *bitch*."

CHAPTER EIGHTEEN

Nico

Elisa: Where are you?

Nico: Getting shitfaced at Woody's

Elisa: Woody's is on 13th? Right?

"This is from that guy over there," the bartender said, sliding a drink toward Nico.

Nico didn't bother to look around, just pushed the drink back.

Last thing he wanted was someone coming on to him. "Tell him thanks, but I'm waiting for my boyfriend."

He had no idea who that would be or when he'd meet this 'boyfriend', but he *was* waiting for him.

Nico took a sip of the bourbon and soda he was nursing.

He probably should go to a straight bar. There all he had to do was avoid looking at the girls and no one would care.

Someone dragged the neighboring stool out. "Two bottles of water, please."

"You came." He knew she would. The bartender returned, and Nico slid a ten across the counter. "I got these. She's my sister."

She nudged one in front of him. "You know you need to alternate to avoid getting sick."

"Thanks." He pushed the tumbler aside and took a drink of water. "But I'm not drunk. That's my first one."

She sniffed his drink. "Good. This smells like straight bourbon."

Nico snorted. "I asked him for a splash of Coke, and he took me literally."

"Sorry, boo, I had just gotten out of the shower when you texted me."

"It's okay. I know you have stuff to do."

"Nothing is more important than being here for you." She pulled him into a one-armed hug. "What happened?"

Nico choked back a sob. "Luke . . . Kent got dumped and he shows up at our door with his luggage. I told him he wasn't welcome, and he said Luke told him he could stay."

He still couldn't believe it. Didn't want to.

"And?"

"I told him he was full of shit. Guess he expected that, 'cause he asked me for my email so he could send me the proof."

"Proof?"

"An email chain from their work accounts. Luke said he could stay. When Kent asked if I'd mind, Luke said he'd talk to me, and I'd be fine."

Elisa sucked in a breath, and he nodded. "I know. He promised me yesterday he wouldn't bring him around. That's what hurts the most. He said he wouldn't. But first time dickwad asks for help . . ." He shrugged.

First time Kent calls, Luke forgets his promise to Nico and sides with Kent.

"Oh, boo." She sniffed and started to cry. "I'm so sorry. I shouldn't have pushed you."

"No." He pulled her closer. "You didn't do that. I did. I wanted to talk to him. You just gave me the nudge I needed."

She shook her head against him. "I did it. You said this would happen, and I told you it wouldn't."

"It's okay." It wasn't. Not even close. "Better I know now."

Elisa leaned back and cradled his face in her hands. "Always the strong one."

Only he wasn't. One wrong word, and he'd be bawling on her shoulder. "I need a favor, E."

"Anything."

"I can't go back there. It hurts too much." In two hours, it went from being the happiest place he could remember to the worst.

"You can stay with me until the wedding."

"Thanks, E. You're the best."

Luke

LUKE AWOKE AFTER A PATCHY, worry-filled sleep to the empty space where Nico should have been sleeping.

Wherever Nico had gone last night, he hadn't come back.

Morning. Midmorning. Afternoon. When the day ended, he raced home. Still not there.

Luke checked his phone for the billionth time, but Nico hadn't read any of the texts he'd sent. He'd tried calling, but it went straight to voicemail.

"Damn." How did things get so fucked-up? Yesterday, he was so sure they were good.

The front door shut.

Luke tensed, stomach somersaulting.

"Nico?" he rushed around the partition and stopped. Not Nico. Elisa. Elisa using Nico's key.

She glared at him in a way that would make Nonna proud. "I'm here to get a few of Nico's things."

Luke blanched, ice spreading through his veins. "You're kidding, right?"

"No, not kidding. And before you start trying to explain, don't. Nico's such an amazing person, and you broke his heart."

Hearing that nearly destroyed Luke, but *he hadn't done it*. "He's got this all wrong, Elisa." He couldn't let her leave without finding some way to get a message to Nico. She was his only link to him.

"Right. He got it wrong." She shook her head. "I can't believe I convinced him to talk to you."

"Elisa—"

"Just stop, Luke. I'm on Nico's side. Always will be."

"Good. Then give me three minutes to prove to you I didn't lie to him." Luke stuffed his shaky hands into his pockets and pulled out his phone. "Here, look."

Nico

Elisa: Where are you?

Nico: Esposito's. Wrapping up for good. Plus checking up on your cake.

Elisa: Esposito's at the Market or the main one on Passyunk?

Nico: Main one. Why?

Elisa: Wait for me, I want to talk.

Nico: Can't we talk when I get to your place?

Elisa: See you soon, boo.

DAMN. So he wouldn't be crashing another night with her?

He pushed his phone into his pocket as Estelle met him at a corner table, an envelope and a sheet of yellow paper in one hand and two cups of coffee in the other. "Thank you so much again for jumping in to help us out so much." She set one coffee in front of him and took the other seat at the table. After taking a sip, she slid the envelope over to him. "Here's your final paycheck."

Nico accepted the envelope and set it aside. "Thank you."

She reached across and squeezed his hand. "You've been a godsend, Nico. I wish you didn't need to leave so soon. I'll miss you."

"I'll miss you too. But it will be good to spend some time at home before school starts." Meaning: he needed to get out of the apartment, permanently. ASAP.

"I'm being selfish."

He snorted. "I'm no prize. Ask my dad."

Estelle laughed. "You know Rocco called him before we hired you. You're a good kid, Nico. The customers loved you."

"I enjoyed it." A lot. "Now's the time to focus on Elisa's wedding."

"Thank you again, sweetie." She patted his hand and slid the yellow paper across the Formica table. "Everything's set. Rocco's going to start on the cake tomorrow, and it will be ready Friday afternoon. We'll deliver it to the Union League first thing Saturday morning."

Nico scanned the invoice, checked the balance owed, and then reached into his backpack for his billfold. "Papà put money in my checking account to cover this, but if you'd rather I use a credit card, I can do that."

"From you, we'll take a check."

He wrote out the check and passed it to her. "Do you mind if I sit for a few minutes? My sister is meeting me here."

"Of course. I'd love to meet her." She patted his hand again and stood. "Thank you again, sweetie. I'm not sure how we'd have managed this summer without you."

"You're welcome."

She marched back behind the counter, and he sipped his coffee, bouncing his leg nervously as he waited for Elisa.

All Nico had to do was get through the next day and a half until his family arrived on Friday. Then he had a ready-made excuse for avoiding Luke. He'd be staying at the hotel with his family. And . . .

He swallowed.

Goddammit. This was why he didn't want to go all in. At least if he'd kept his distance, he wouldn't feel so worthless again.

He slammed his eyes shut. Who was he kidding? No matter how it ended, it was going to hurt, but at least he wouldn't have known Luke didn't want him.

The bell tinkled, and his sister entered the shop. He forced a smile but dropped it when he saw Luke slinking in behind her, looking as miserable as Nico felt.

"*Seriously*, Elisa?" He'd *told* her he couldn't face Luke. "After everything I did for you this summer?"

"I know, boo, but before you lose your shit, you need to listen."

"Fuck that. I'm outta here."

She blocked his path and put her hand on his chest. "No, you're going to listen. When I say I love you to the moon and back, I mean it. You need to hear what *really* happened."

"What really happened is he told Kent he could stay."

"No, boo. He didn't. I checked out his story. It's true."

"What?" Nico's knees nearly gave out. He inched back and plopped onto his chair. "You checked? With who?"

"That's for Luke to say." She framed his face with her hands. "Just hear him out. If you still feel the same, you can come stay the next two days. But I don't think that's gonna happen."

She smiled and pulled her hands back. "You two talk while I go check on my wedding cake."

Luke needed a push from Elisa to move closer. Shuffling his feet, he slowly took the seat across from Nico. They watched each other until Nico couldn't stand the silence. "I'm listening."

Not the friendliest opening, but despite what E said, he still hurt.

"Nico, I'm so sorry you're hurt, but I swear I didn't send those emails. Kent did."

"Kent?"

"I was talking to Coury about how he had the balls to ask me to stay and how I said no. I thought I heard someone outside my door, but I didn't check at first. After I told Coury how I promised you I wouldn't bring him around you, Kent walks in and says he needs to speak to me. He wouldn't leave, so *I* left. I . . . I never locked my computer."

He wanted to believe it, but believing left him shattered. "And how did E check this out?"

"I left to call Coury back." He pulled out his phone. "I called him at 11:09 from outside the building. When I told her this, she told me to call Coury and give her the phone. She grilled him for a few minutes and then asked how she could help."

Nico squeezed his eyes shut. The emotional Ping Pong match he was living left him disoriented. Luke touched his hand.

"Nico, I swear, I didn't send those emails. I meant every word I said to you on Monday. I want you. Just you. All of you. The way you want to be. No filters, no changes. I know it looks like I betrayed you, but . . ."

"You didn't." He opened his eyes and felt a new clarity. "I believe you."

"You do?" Luke sounded as relieved as he looked.

Nico nodded. "After spending the summer with you, it's easier to believe you than those emails." He turned his head toward his sister. "And if you could convince *her*, you must be telling the truth."

Luke got up and launched himself at Nico. "Oh God, thank you." He crushed Nico in a bear hug.

"I'm sorry, Luke. I should have given you a chance to explain." He should have done so many things different during the summer.

"Please don't be sorry. I almost believed I sent those emails." He let out a giddy laugh. "You warned me that first day when we drove from Harrison."

Nico put his fingers on Luke's lips. "Shh. I don't want to see *or* talk about him anymore."

"Right. But I need to see him again. At least one more time."

"Don't hit him, Luke. He's not worth it."

Luke grinned. "Hitting him won't be as satisfying as what's about to drop on him."

"What are you up to?"

Luke

Luke: Can you come to my office?

Kent: Planning to apologize for being a dickwad to me?

Luke: Something like that.

"Okay, I'm here," Kent said before he stepped through the threshold to Luke's office. "Let the apologies—"

Luke almost found the deflated expression worth the angst Kent had caused Nico. Not quite, but it was a start.

"Hello, Kent," Chris said. "Please come in."

Luke's small office was crowded, but everyone stood at the edges to leave room for Kent.

"What's going on?"

"Something unusual happened on Monday that I need your help with."

"Monday?" Kent shot Luke a plea for help as the noose tightened.

Fat chance. "You remember, the day you refused to leave my office when I was trying to talk to my roommate. That Monday."

"Um. Okay."

"So. Luke told us someone used his email without his authorization at around 11:10 a.m."

"He mentioned that."

"I asked the IT department to run a diagnostic of his computer." Chris pointed to the guy seated behind Luke's desk.

"I ran the IP address and found that two different firm emails were used at the same time from this terminal. One using the desktop Outlook app, the other using the web-based version." He spun the screen around so everyone in the room could see. "Luke's email was using the desktop app. Your email, Mr. Waller, was using web-based Outlook."

"Luke was using my email account?" Kent's voice shook, and Luke snorted.

"Nice try." Chris nodded to someone in a suit. "Mr. Young?"

"At your request, Mr. Rayner, I reviewed the security footage. Mr. DeRosa was seen exiting the building at 11:08 a.m. He didn't return until 11:32 a.m. carrying a Panera Bread bag. We also pulled the floor lobby video and Mr. Waller entered this suite at 11:02 a.m. He left at 11:14 a.m., one minute after the last email was sent from this terminal."

"Thank you." Chris turned his attention on Kent. "Using another employee's email without authorization is grounds for termination."

"I didn't send those emails. Someone else must have done it."

"No one else sent them. You did." Chris nodded toward Mr. Young. "We spoke to Nico, who told us how you arrived at his and

Luke's apartment and showed him these emails. You said they were from Luke. Since both emails were written on this terminal, your claim that someone used your account lacks credibility. In fact, your admission inculpates you in the unauthorized use of Luke's account.

"Your internship is terminated. Mr. Young will escort you back to your cubicle, where you will collect your personal belongings, turn over your ID badge, and then vacate the premises. You are also barred from entering this building without further written notice."

He flicked two fingers, and Mr. Young motioned for Kent to leave. Sparing a last angry stare at Luke, Kent shrugged away from Mr. Young's grasp and walked out of the office.

The IT guy left, leaving Luke with his managing partner. When Chris didn't leave, Luke knew what was coming next. It wasn't how he'd expected the summer to end. He had regrets, but not for making sure Kent answered for what he'd done.

"I'll get my things and leave my badge here, Chris." He dug the hard plastic rectangle out of his pocket and set it on the desk. "Thank you for everything, and I'm truly sorry for what happened."

Chris nodded and headed toward the door. Instead of leaving, he swung it shut. When he turned, he motioned for Luke to take his seat.

His legs were like jelly, so sitting wasn't hard. Chris still hadn't said anything as he used Luke's other chair. Crossing his arms over his chest, he said back. "You think you're being terminated as well?"

"I can't imagine the firm has time for this kind of petty stuff."

"You didn't need to tell me. Had you kept quiet, we'd never have found out."

And Kent would have gotten away with it. But that wasn't his motivation. "Nico needed to know the truth."

"Nico?" Chris raised an eyebrow. "Not the firm?"

"The firm does too, but I'd be lying to you if I said that was my motivation." It might have saved his internship if he'd lied. "Kent really hurt Nico with this deception."

Chris uncrossed his arms, reached forward, and picked up Luke's badge. "You're right about the firm not wanting to deal with drama. Any time an accountant is making waves, it generally isn't good news. Our clients prefer we be noticed as little as possible."

Luke swallowed the bile rising in his throat as Chris turned Luke's ID card around and around. Telling his parents he'd wasted his summer was going suck. Even more so when he told them it was a failure in part due to Kent.

"But they also prize integrity." Luke snapped his gaze back to Chris's. "It's one of the hardest traits for us to measure during the summer program, because it's rarely an issue."

He tossed the badge in Luke's direction. It skidded across the hard surface and into Luke's lap.

"Go home and relax tonight." He smiled as he stood. "I'll see you tomorrow. Oh, and Luke?"

"Yes?"

"How about you and Nico come for dinner next weekend? The kids keep asking about you."

Luke swallowed a sigh of relief. "Let me check with Nico."

LUKE STOPPED HALFWAY up the stairs. The aroma coming from their apartment had him salivating.

Nico was home.

Thank God.

"Nico?" he called as soon as he shut the door.

"In the kitchen."

Where else? Smiling, Luke moved around the wall to find Nico working in front of the stove. "Smells great. What is it?"

"Spaghetti aglio e olio. Which is spaghetti with olive oil and garlic." Nico stirred the garlic in the frying pan with a wooden spoon. "Along with lots of fresh parsley and pine nuts. Nonna makes hers with anchovies, but I like it without."

They looked at each other, wordlessly acknowledging Nico's absence. How he'd run. Luke caught a glimmer of fragile uncertainty in Nico's eyes and smiled gently.

"Really? You don't like Nonna's cooking?"

"Shush." Nico waved the spoon at Luke, smiling. A real smile that made Luke's heart skip. "Trust me, you'll be glad I left them out. They make it too fishy."

"I'll take your word for it." He leaned in for a kiss, and Nico didn't disappoint him. It reeked of the domestic bliss he'd glimpsed all summer. "Let me change, and I'll help you."

"It's almost done, but thanks." It looked like Nico had it under control. He always did.

"Okay. I'll be right out."

He quickly changed into khaki shorts and a salmon polo shirt. His stomach rumbled, and he emerged in record time. Nico, however, wasn't in the kitchen. "Nico?"

"Here."

Luke turned left, and Nico held out a black tux. "What's that?"

"I went to Cantangello's to get my tux today." That being the tailor Rocco Esposito recommended when they needed tuxedoes for the charity event. "Funny thing. They gave me two."

Nico pulled the second one from behind the first.

"Really?" He smiled and stepped closer. "Funny how these things always seem to happen to you."

Nico held one out. "Would you believe I asked them to ready one for you?"

"Why would you do that?"

"Because I was hoping you'd be my date to my sister's

wedding." He moved into Luke's personal space. "Would you please go with me, Luke?"

"I'd love to be your date to the wedding, and everything else you want us to do."

Nico put the suits down and wrapped his hands around Luke's waist. "Oh, Mr. DeRosa. You say the darndest things."

CHAPTER NINETEEN

Luke

Luke: Hey. What are you doing?

Coury: Aren't you at a wedding with your pretend boyfriend?

Luke: Nope. At a wedding with my real boyfriend!

Coury: FINALLY! Congrats!

Nico

Nico: So maybe you were right.

Isaiah: I hope that means what I think it means.

Nico: I'm in love with Luke.

Isaiah: Duh.

Nico: And he loves me too

Isaiah: I KNEW IT

Nico had done it.

The wedding went off without a hitch. The photos had been taken, the reception was in full swing, the band was playing, and everyone was jolly. *Happy*.

Nico scanned the crowd and stopped when he saw his father and Luke laughing at something Joey had said. Luke fit with his family like he'd known them forever. And because Nico's family loved him, they accepted Luke like he'd been one of them just as long.

God, he hoped this lasted.

No. He didn't need to hope.

It was real.

His father glanced in Nico's direction, and the others followed his gaze. Nico waved and headed toward the kitchen to check on when they would serve the cake.

Two minutes later, he was back in the main hall.

"Nico," Giuseppe Amato said from behind him. "I was looking or you."

"Papà. Why aren't you schmoozing with the guests? Or better yet, spending time with the bride?"

"Because I'm trying to track down my elusive son to thank him for all his hard work." He put his hand on Nico's left shoulder. "I'll admit, I had my doubts when Elisa told me you were taking over."

"I wasn't going to let E down."

"That alone should have told me you would do a wonderful job." His father kept his grip on Nico's shoulder. Just before the moment got awkward, he nodded. "Your mother and I plan to give you the rest of the fee we would have paid the planner."

"You don't need to do that, Papà."

Giuseppe smiled. "Always the good son. But this is a gift. You did this for your sister and she . . . we *all* . . . appreciate what you did. You keep it and use it when you get your own place."

Nico couldn't swallow the lump in his throat. Unable to speak, he hugged his father.

"You deserve it, Nico." He rubbed Nico's back gently. "I'm very proud of you, for so many reasons. Just one more thing I can brag about."

"Thank you, Papà." Nico wiped his eyes and stepped back. "Thank you."

"You're welcome." He glanced over Nico's shoulder. "Luke is a wonderful person. Your mother and I are so glad you found someone to make you happy."

Nico's stomach somersaulted. "Papà, I am. Nerve-wrackingly so."

Giuseppe held up his hands. "I know it's too soon to say such things, but everyone likes him."

Nico's heart pounded. "That's good, because I *really* like him." His gaze caught on Luke approaching.

"I can tell." Giuseppe squeezed Luke's shoulder as he walked away.

"Hey, stranger."

Luke looked gorgeous in his tuxedo, and Nico's heart skipped. "Having fun?"

"Not as much as I *could* be having. My date has been avoiding me." Luke winked. "But I'm hopeful the night will pick up."

"Right. I'm such a hot commodity today."

"Definitely hot." He leaned in and kissed Nico's cheek. "Will you dance with me?"

Nico touched his cheek, the touch of Luke's soft lips lingering. "I have . . . stuff to do."

"Actually, you don't." Luke took Nico's hand and nodded toward the dance floor. "I spoke to the banquet manager while you were talking to your dad. The only thing left is the cake, and that'll happen after the tables are set for dessert."

Luke's information was correct. "You're plotting something."

"Yes. I'm plotting to dance with you."

Luke led them to an empty space close to where Elisa was dancing with Elliott. Lively music shifted to a slow dance.

"Perfect timing." Luke waggled his eyebrows and draped his arms warmly over Nico's shoulders. Nico breathed in Luke's clean, soapy scent and wrapped his arms around Luke's waist. Luke's heat blazed against Nico, making his breath snag.

Luke swayed with him, met his gaze and didn't let up.

"You and your brother are so different. Joey's so serious."

"He's a doctor. I guess it comes with the job."

"Yeah, maybe. And why do I feel like I met Nico age seven last night?"

"Elijah?" He hadn't seen his nephew since Christmas, but Elijah had practically vaulted into his arms when he arrived. "I don't know what you're talking about."

"Sure you don't." Luke winked. "He sure loves his uncle Nico."

"The feelings are mutual."

"You'll make a great dad one day."

Nico rubbed his nape. "You were pretty good with the kids too."

"I love children. I hope to have my own someday."

That just made Luke even more perfect. "I had no idea."

"Now you do."

Nico's senses were short-circuiting. He tightened his hold on Luke's waist, and glanced to his left. Seeing his sister so happy made him teary eyed.

"What's wrong?"

Nico blinked quickly to clear his eyes. "Nothing's wrong. I'm .

. ." He caught himself. "I usually cry at weddings. This being E's, I've cried more than usual."

Luke leaned in and whispered into Nico's ear. "Feel free to cry on my shoulder whenever you need to."

Nico closed his eyes and rested his head on Luke's shoulder. "Thank you."

They stayed like that, swaying slightly, until someone tapped him on the shoulder.

"May I cut in?" Elisa slipped beside them in her dazzling white dress.

Nico stepped back so she could dance with Luke.

They each smacked one of his arms. "What? I figured you were tired of me by now."

"No way, boo. Not happening." She smiled at Luke. "I know you've been waiting all day to dance with him, but so have I. Do you mind sharing him for a few minutes?"

"Just a few. Then I want him back." Luke backed away, grinning.

Nico took his sister's hand and made small moves that barely qualified as dancing.

"First, thank you." She kissed his right cheek. "Today was everything I wanted. And you made it happen."

"Meh. It was mostly done when I got here."

She squeezed his hand tight and shook her head. "Nope. You don't get to do that. You did this for me, boo. I won't forget."

He scanned the ballroom until he locked eyes with Luke. Nico's pulse raced. "Coming to Philly worked out pretty good for me, too."

"Good. I want you to be happy, boo." Tears formed around the edges of her eyes. "Will you do that for me?"

Nico blinked back the heat in his eyes. "How is that something for you?"

"Because I love *you* a hundred googolplex times." They both laughed at her nine-year-old comeback. "Promise me you'll try with Luke?" The song changed, and she led them into a quick dance. "You fit well together."

They did fit together. "I promise."

Her face lit up, and he spun her around once. While she twirled, he motioned with his eyes for Elliott to take over. The groom didn't need to be asked twice.

"Thanks for thinking of me on your day." He kissed her cheek and handed her back to her new husband.

She winked. "Every day is family day."

He couldn't argue with that.

Threading through dancers, he made his way toward the guy he planned to start his own family with.

The thousand-watt smile on Luke's face burned away any doubts Nico might have had left. Luke wanted him.

He took Luke's hand and kissed him chastely. "God, I wish I could kiss you more. Like, obscenely more."

"Soon." Luke's grip shifted on his hip and he leaned toward his ear. "I might have gotten a key to your suite from Elisa. And I might have put my stuff in there."

Nico pulled back, snorting. "And I might have given you my bag to take with you."

Luke entwined their fingers and turned back to the dance floor. "Can I tell you something?"

"You can tell me anything."

"I didn't know what it meant to be in love until I met you."

Nico slowly faced him, and Luke gazed back.

"It's all the little things you do. You care about me and make me feel special. You never said it, but I knew. Because you showed me. Every day. That's why I love you, Nico Amato."

"I love you too, Luke." As the staff cleared the tables, the weight of his wedding planner title vanished. He was free. No more duties. Well, none other than be ridiculously happy with Luke.

The guests seemed to sense something was happening and

most of them left the dance floor. Including his nonna. On the arm of his cousin, CJ.

"Up for meeting another family member?"

"I thought I met all the important ones already."

"Just one more. I want you to meet my cousin CJ."

"Ah, the infamous CJ. What's CJ short for?"

He took Luke's hand and lead him across the room. "Carmine, Jr., but he hates Carmine, so stick to CJ."

When his cousin spotted them, he waved. After making sure Nonna was in her seat, he circled the table and met them halfway.

"Nico!" He threw open his arms for a hug.

After they thumped each other's backs in front of an amused Luke, Nico stepped back.

"CJ, this is my boyfriend, Luke."

"Nice to meet you." Luke held out his hand, but CJ went for a hug.

"Hey, hey." Nico tapped him on the back. "Get your own boyfriend."

"I kind of do, but Mom and Dad would've had a cow if I brought him."

"Really?" Luke looked at Nico, who nodded. "Sorry. I shouldn't have asked."

"It's okay." CJ shrugged, but Nico knew it *wasn't* fine. "I'm staying at Nonno and Nonna's"

Nico knew his cousin had spent the last month with his parents and grandparents. "Are you going home after the wedding?"

"No. I told Mom and Dad yesterday."

"Ah, that would explain why they aren't sitting with Nonno and Nonna."

"Yeah." CJ frowned. "It wasn't pleasant, but Nonno raised his voice, and Mom threw her hands up and walked away."

"Nonno yelled at someone?" Luke sounded stunned.

"Exactly." CJ nodded.

"Good." It *was* good. CJ needed to get away from his overly religious father. Nico squeezed his cousin's shoulder. "We need to go see Nonna."

"Yeah, you do. She's been fussing at everyone that you're working too hard."

Nico laughed and reached for Luke's hand. It already felt so normal.

"Nonna, you look amazing." Nico kissed her on the cheek, "And you were really dancing with CJ."

Nonna opened for a hug. After kissing him on both cheeks, she swatted him in the head.

"What's that for?"

She pointed a finger at him. "Don't you ever lie to me again, you hear?"

He rubbed his head and sent the chuckling Luke a playful growl. "Huh?"

Nonna turned her finger on Luke. "You too." She waved him into a hug and smacked his head.

Nico swallowed a nervous giggle.

"What'd we do?"

"Tomasso Merighi?" Her evil eye set Nico back a step.

"What . . .?"

"Did you think I didn't notice Luca wasn't your boyfriend from the spring?"

"How . . .?"

"Never you mind how I know."

Luke slipped his fingers between Nico's. "Yes, Nonna. Nico and I promise not to do it again."

"I should hope not." She finally smiled. It had an edge to it that frightened Nico. "Tomasso's grandmother asked me how you were doing since her grandson broke up with you. I told her you and Luca were so happy, you never mentioned it."

Nico snorted, then it grew into a full laugh.

"*Rozzo.*" She tossed up her hands and flicked them when she brought them down.

"What?" Luke whispered in his ear.

He took advantage of the closeness to nick a kiss. "Uncouth. Why didn't you say anything earlier?" Nico asked, flushed.

"Because I sensed the spark and knew you'd come to your senses." She eyed them closely, and Luke blushed just as hard as Nico was. "And it looks like you have."

Someone in the hall started tapping their knife to their glass as Elisa and Elliott reached the head table. The family took up the call. Even Elliott's family seemed into the moment.

Elisa rolled her eyes but didn't seem too put off as she kissed Elliott. All the happy couples followed suit. Luke leaned in, and Nico closed the distance, smiling into the kiss.

He pulled back and stared into Luke's eyes. "The first of many more to come. Better get used to it."

Luke linked their fingers. "I'm totally down with this tradition."

EPILOGUE

Christmas Day – Iowa

Luke

Luke: Made it home safely.

Nonna: Good. Have fun. We'll miss you.

Luke carried his bag up the stairs and beckoned Nico to follow. Flying on Christmas Day was much better than leaving earlier. The whole arrangement had been perfect.

Nico hadn't lied when he said Christmas Eve was a bigger deal for his family. Elisa and Elliott were there and took the train to Philadelphia to spend Christmas with his family. She was training him well.

Luke stopped by his room first and dumped his bag, then led Nico to the guest room. His mom had made it up, put towels on the bed and a new comforter.

Nico plopped his bag down and tugged Luke into a soft kiss. "Merry Christmas, sweetie." Nico reached for his backpack and pulled out an envelope.

"What?" They'd exchanged gifts at the Amatos' last night.

"It's customary to *open* gifts you're given and not ask what they are."

Keeping his dark, twinkly gaze on Nico, Luke slid his finger under the flap and pried it open. He pulled out three slips of paper and shifted through them.

"Is it customary to guess what it is after you open it?"

Nico kissed him again and grabbed the sheets of paper. He held up a menu from Esposito's Bakery. "My family bought Esposito's from Rocco. He's staying on for at least three years to help train someone to run it for the family."

Something in the way Nico said that thrilled Luke.

"This is a picture of Mrs. R's house. Quinton and his girlfriend are moving out after the spring semester. So the apartment is available to rent come June."

"What? Why?"

Nico put a finger on his lips. "Last is a Phillies' schedule. I thought we'd catch a few games this year after you move there."

Luke had only gotten a job offer the week before school ended. He had until January 15 to accept. "This is sweet, but what's going on?"

"My father wants me to take over Esposito's and learn from Rocco. CJ is coming too."

"You're moving to Philly?" This wasn't real. "What about your family and the bakery?"

Nico held Luke's shaking hands. "You're going to be my family. You, and however many kids we have."

"Are you . . ."

"Sure?"

Luke nodded.

"I'll be running Esposito's—and it'll be at least fifteen years before Papà is ready to retire. We have plenty of time to figure out if you want to transfer to New York, or we stay in Philly."

We! Nico kept throwing out that word. "Nico . . . this is amazing. But you can't give up your family."

"I'm not. Not only is Elisa in Philly, I'll need to be in New York a lot—but most of that can be on weekends. As you know, Amato Railways gets you pretty close to my house."

"Just don't drink the radiator fluid."

"Exactly. Second, my father wants me in Philly to run the new shop. He has big plans to expand. So we have gobs of time to sort that out."

Luke was numb. He'd never mentioned how anxious he was about what would happen after graduation, but somehow Nico knew. "You did this didn't you?"

"*Omertà*." He put his fingers to his lips. "If that doesn't work, I'm invoking the Fifth."

"C'mon, Nico, we need to talk about this."

"Honestly, I want this. I want *you*. Always. It won't be enough seeing each other on weekends. I want to come home and make dinner for you and ask about your day when you come home. I want to share silly customer stories with you and gripe about the price of flour.

"We can worry about where we live in ten years, nine years from now. For now, I have a job in Philly, you have a job in Philly, and we have a place in Philly."

"What about the second-rate farmers' markets?"

"Love is more important?"

"And your made-up Brooklyn language? Are you prepared to give that up?"

"I view this as an opportunity to spread diversity and teach Philly a few things."

Luke snorted. "You're okay living in a cozy one-bedroom with an inadequately stocked kitchen?"

"Nope. But we're not living in the apartment. CJ is."

"CJ's going to live in our apartment with us?"

"Interesting choice of words, our apartment." Nico found the picture of Mrs. R's house and flipped it over.

"It's for sale?"

"No. It's been sold already."

Luke stared at the page for a moment. A thought bubbled up. "Wait. You bought it?"

Nico chuckled. "I wish. My parents bought it. We'll be renting from them. They said we could buy it from them once we get settled."

Luke drew Nico against him. "I can't make you give up everything for me. I'm sure I'll find a job in New York."

"I'm not giving up anything for you. This is for us. Plus, how many twenty-two-year-olds are going to be running a multi-million-dollar business right out of college? If we went to New York, I'd be in Papà's shadow until he retires. This gives me time to shine."

Luke bumped their foreheads together.

"A lot can happen in ten years," Nico said. "You might hate working for a firm, you may find a new job, we may love Philly and not want to move, we might hate Philly and both want to move. The only constant in that is we'll do it together."

Luke caressed Nico's face. This was happening. They were happening. "Together?"

Nico kissed him. "Together."

~ The End ~

BETTER TO BELIEVE

We're working on new installment(s) in the Harrison Campus Series. Next up is Luke's roommate, Coury Henderson.

You met Coury before Luke and Nico left for Philadelphia, and got to know him a bit through his texts to Luke. This will be his story.

[Note: This snippet is not final and is a subject to change.]

Chapter One

Coury

Balls zipped across the field house floor and smacked into well-oiled leather, and Coury Henderson breathed it all in from the bleachers.

Baseball.

It should be him down there practicing.

His roommate Luke jumped up for a ball way over his head and yelled lighthearted smack for the errant throw.

That curse should have been directed at Coury.

Since that first awkward practice freshman year, they'd

warmed up together. They'd talked up today all last semester. They'd been impatient to slip their fingers into the well-worn groves of their gloves.

Coury closed his eyes and felt the ache in his side—and the heavier one in his chest.

Luke had warned him not to go snowboarding . . .

The metal bleacher rattled and jounced at the arrival of another spectator.

"Here you are." Nico set a travel mug of coffee next to Coury's leg. "Two sugars and a splash of cream."

Coury smiled as he tapped fists with Luke's boyfriend. "Thanks, Nero."

"Anytime, Cokey." Nico sat and stretched his long legs onto the bench below. He eyed the phone Coury gripped in his good hand. "Please tell me you're not texting that awful being."

"Nope, I took your advice and deleted her from my phone and unfollowed her on social media." Hailey dumping him had hurt, but it was nothing to the prospect of not playing baseball this season . . . "I don't even know that she and mister richy pants just got back from the South of France yesterday."

Nico snorted. "Forgot one?"

"Twitter." He'd blocked her right after he saw all the happy photos.

His phone dinged. "Finally." At Nico's suspicious brow, Coury grinned. "Not Hailey, Liam."

"Oh him, your best friend." Nico pouted, and Coury rolled his eyes.

"Best and longest friend."

"Go on then, bemuse yourself with him."

{Liam: Seriously, Bro? It's the middle of the night.}

Coury smiled at the goofy bed hair his best friend probably sported as his sleepy eyes read his message. Served him right for sending drunken, cryptic texts at 2:00 a.m. The *real* middle of the night.

{Coury: Be glad I didn't call.}

{Liam: Why are you up at 7 fucking 30 on a SUNDAY!}

{Coury: First practice.}

Not a real practice, just a bunch of guys working the rust off before the university officially allowed to start. But, unofficial meant scheduling fieldhouse time that no one else wanted.

{Liam: You're playing?}

{Coury: Just watching.}

{Coury: Now that you're up, what did you need to tell me?}

{Liam: Dude! Why are you watching?}

{Coury: News or I'm putting the phone away.}

{Liam: Beckett's come home from Texas and is living near Harrison.}

Beckett? Tall, dark, brooding Beckett who'd set his twelve-year-old hormones on fire, Beckett? Beckett who'd clued him in that he was bisexual?

Huh.

"Are you all right, darling?" Nico leaned over and read Coury's screen. "Who's this Beckett that has you all hot and bothered?"

Coury snatched his phone away. "Didn't anyone tell you it's bad manners to read people's messages?"

"Tons, but I do it anyway." He leaned back and took a sip. "One can't gossip properly without accurate information."

Coury pointed warningly at his friend. "Don't you fuckin dare."

A ball clanked in the bleacher below. Luke jogged toward them it was Nico's turn to flush. God those two were in love.

"Hey, sweetie." Luke bounced up the aluminum bleachers and gave Nico a peck on the lips. He gently pried the coffee from his hand and took a sip, "How'd you get Mr. Cranky here to smile?" Luke said with a nod to Coury.

"Not my charms, sadly. Some guy called Beckett did that."

"Beckett?" Luke took another drink and gave it back to his boyfriend. "Who's Beckett?"

"Liam's older brother," Coury said. "He played in the Houston

Astro organization?" He rolled his eyes at Nico and Luke's unsubtle grinning exchange. "Please, he's straight and he's Liam's brother."

"Right because no one *ever* lusted after their best friend's older brother," Nico said, and gestured Luke toward the field. "You need to go, babe. Someone's getting his jock in a bunch."

Luke winked and ran off, leaving Coury staring wistfully after him.

Nico patted Coury's arm. "You'll be out there soon."

"Right." *Hopefully.*

"When can you start again?"

"I see the doctor Wednesday. Assuming things are good, I go to rehab for four weeks."

"So . . . you had a thing for this Beckett?" Nico asked.

"When I was *twelve.* He was the best player to come from our town that anyone could remember. More like I idolized him and wanted to be like him. Haven't seen him in nine years."

"Gotcha."

Someone yelled on the field and Coury looked up.

"Whomever Luke is warming up with can't hit the side of the barn from inside," Nico said.

"Look at you," Coury said with a big grin. "Six months with Luke and your Mr. Baseball now."

"As much time as I've spent listening to you two talk, what did you expect?"

He bumped shoulders. Nico made Luke happy. Happier than Coury had ever seen. That alone made him good people.

{Liam: Hello! You better not ditch me after waking me up.}

{Coury: Sorry, was talking to someone. That's cool your bro is coming back.}

{Liam: He's stayin with g-pa. I gave him your number.}

{Coury: My number?}

{Liam: Because he doesn't know anyone under 75. Figured you two could hang out in between my visits.}

{Coury: So you'll visit B, but not me?}

Three seconds later his phone rang. Liam's name flashed on the screen.

Nico slapped the bench and stood. "Be right back. Gonna use the men's room."

"Hello?"

"He needs a friend, bro," Liam said. "Last few years were rough for him. You're a familiar face until he gets settled."

"I mean, he probably doesn't remember me."

"Probably a good thing. You really filled out with age."

Coury rolled his eyes.

"So you'll hang with him?" Liam asked.

"Sure."

Luke fielded a sharp ground ball and zinged it to the first baseman. It hit the guys outstretched mitt with a snap.

God he ached to be out there.

"Stop torturing yourself," Liam said softly. "And, thanks. You're the best, C-man."

ABOUT ANDY

Andy Gallo prefers mountains over the beach, coffee over tea, and regardless if you shake it or stir it, he isn't drinking a martini. He remembers his "good old days" as filled with mullets, disco music, too-short shorts, and too-high socks. Thanks to good shredders and a lack of social media, there is no proof he ever descended into any of those evils.

Married and living his own happy every after, Andy helps others find their happy endings in the pages of his stories. No living or deceased ex-boyfriends appear on the pages of his stories.

Andy and his husband of more than twenty-five years spend their days raising their daughter and rubbing elbows with other parents. Embracing his status as the gay dad, Andy sometimes has to remind others that one does want a hint of color even when chasing after their child.

Join my Facebook group for more of your favorite characters and to meet new favorites:

https://www.facebook.com/groups/GalloreousReaders/

Contact Andy:

www.andygallo.com
andy@andygallo.com
www.facebook.com/andygalloauthor
https://twitter.com/AuthorAndyGallo

ABOUT ANYTA

A bit about me: I'm a big, BIG fan of slow-burn romances. I love to read and write stories with characters who slowly fall in love.

Some of my favorite tropes to read and write are: Enemies to Lovers, Friends to Lovers, Clueless Guys, Bisexual, Pansexual, Demisexual, Oblivious MCs, Everyone (Else) Can See It, Slow Burn, Love Has No Boundaries.

I write a variety of stories, Contemporary MM Romances with a good dollop of angst, Contemporary lighthearted MM Romances, and even a splash of fantasy.
My books have been translated into German, Italian, French, and Thai.

Contact: http://www.anytasunday.com/about-anyta/
Sign up for Anyta's newsletter and receive a free e-book: http://www.anytasunday.com/newsletter-free-e-book/

Join my Facebook group to chat all things Slow Burn Romance:
https://www.facebook.com/groups/SlowBurnSundays/

You can also find me here:
www.anytasunday.com
anytasunday@gmail.com

Made in the USA
Coppell, TX
10 April 2021

53442005R00142